PRAISE FOR N

#1 Essence Bestselling author

"Always surprising, Nikki Turner's prose moves like a Porsche, switching gears from tender to vicious in an instant."
—50 Cent

"Nikki Turner has once again taken street literature to the next level, further proving that she is indeed 'The Queen of Hip-Hop Fiction.'"
—Zane, author of *Dear G-Spot*

"Another vivid slice of street life from Nikki Turner. You can't go wrong with this page-turner!"
—T.I. on *Ghetto Superstar*

"Few writers working in the field today bring the drama quite as dramatically as Nikki Turner. . . . [She's] a master at weaving juicy, 'hood-rich sagas of revenge, regret, and redemption."
—Vibe.com on *Forever a Hustler's Wife*

"USDA hood certified."
—Teri Woods, author of the *True to the Game* trilogy on *Riding Dirty on I-95*

ALSO BY NIKKI TURNER

NOVELS

Relapse

Ghetto Superstar

Black Widow

Forever a Hustler's Wife

Death Before Dishonor
(with 50 Cent)

Riding Dirty on I-95

The Glamorous Life

A Project Chick

A Hustler's Wife

EDITOR

Street Chronicles: Backstage

Street Chronicles: Christmas in the Hood

Street Chronicles: Girls in the Game

Street Chronicles: Tales from da Hood
(contributing author)

CONTRIBUTING AUTHOR

Girls from da Hood

Girls from da Hood 2

The Game: Short Stories About the Life

Natural Born Hustler

Nikki Turner

Natural Born Hustler

A NOVEL

ONE WORLD TRADE PAPERBACKS
BALLANTINE BOOKS NEW YORK

Natural Born Hustler is a work of fiction. Names, characters, places, and incidents are the products of the author's imagination or are used fictitiously. Any resemblance to actual events, locales, or persons, living or dead, is entirely coincidental.

A One World Trade Paperback Original

Published in the United States by One World Books, an imprint of The Random House Publishing Group, a division of Random House, Inc., New York.

LIBRARY OF CONGRESS CATALOGING-IN-PUBLICATION DATA

Turner, Nikki.
Natural born hustler : a novel / Nikki Turner.
p. cm.
ISBN 978-0-345-52360-0 (pbk.)
1. African Americans—Fiction. 2. Street life—Fiction.
3. Urban fiction. I. Title.
PS3620.U7659N38 2010
813'.6—dc22 2010022021

Printed in the United States of America

www.oneworldbooks.net

2 4 6 8 9 7 5 3 1

Book design by Laurie Jewell

This book is dedicated to my auntie,
very best friend, and sister,
Yvonne Murray-Lewis.
You are such a phenomenal woman
with so many talents.
I treasure you for all the secrets
you hold, laughs we share,
the words of wisdom and inspiration
you give—they go such a long way.

And
to all the natural born hustlers on
planet Earth: You know who you are—
whether you want to admit it or not.

A Special Message from Nikki Turner to Her Readers

Dear Loyal Readers,

When my publisher suggested that I pen a third addition to the epic Hustler's Wife series, I was delighted by the idea, but I knew it wouldn't be easy. This new novel would have to walk in the footsteps of two hugely successful predecessors—*A Hustler's Wife* and *Forever a Hustler's Wife.* The original characters, Yarni and Des, are both well into their thirties, a bit too mature to be running around doing some of the crazy stuff that I usually like to write about!

Nevertheless I accepted the task and in the process I created this amazing, multi-dimensional, and complex teenage female character, Desember. She was a fatherless child who had so much heart and spunk that her persona began to dominate the project. It quickly became obvious to me that Desember needed her own book. As a reader (because I feel I'm a reader first), I felt we needed to delve deeper into her past and background and care more about her before she made her debut in the third installment of *A Hustler's Wife*. And I knew just how to pitch it to the people that could get Desember's story on the shelves and into your hands.

When I called my agent, Marc, and shared my newest bright idea with him about a novel that would serve as a bridge between the second and third novel in the series, he was excited about the vision. (He keeps calling the book Hustler's Wife 2½, which is why we don't let Marc come up with the titles.)

Now all we had to do was to sell the idea to my longtime editor and friend, Melody, at One World/Ballantine. At first Melody thought it was an okay idea. After she read the outline she began to like the idea a little more; the story was becoming contagious. And before the entire journey had run its course, Melody, like me, had fallen in love with Desember.

Once my publisher and agent got the behind-the-scenes business done, I found out that *Natural Born Hustler* would be a fall release—my first ever. Up until now, all of my novels have been published in the summer. I can't begin to count the letters and emails I've received from you, my readers, expressing how hard it is to wait an entire year between novels, so I knew that you would love this.

But wait, I still needed to write the book. It was no joke, I was under the gun in the worst way, but I loved every minute of it. Maybe it was because Desember's spunk reminded me so much of myself (many, many years ago). Growing up, I was also estranged from my father, and I'd always longed to know him and for him to know the real me. Ironically after I had finished writing this book, my father called me and apologized for the years apart and vowed to do all he could to build a better bond.

I had a great male role model in my grandfather, who, along with my grandmother, raised me. He was the absolute best and did a phenomenal job with me, but there is nothing like the bond between a father and a daughter. I'm eager to see how our relationship develops.

Sorry for my digression. I didn't mean to get so personal but if I can't share this with you, my loyal readers, then who can I? Anyway, there were times in this book when I would stop and laugh and read aloud, and on a few occasions I would even speak out loud to the characters. This was unusual because my characters speak to me all the time, but it's rare I find myself reversing the roles.

I had too much fun writing this book. I know it was supposed to be a treat for you but it was a real delight for me! Desember is one of the most unforgettable female protagonists that I've created since the infamous Yarni of *A Hustler's Wife.* And I'm willing to bet the farm that once you read her story and get to know her, you will love her too!

Now, with no further ado . . . here's my newest baby, *Natural Born Hustler*.

Enjoy!

Much Love,
Nikki Turner

Natural Born Hustler

Prologue

Desember Day fumbled for the key to her mother's house and upon entering, she heard her mother and stepfather in the midst of an argument, which wasn't unusual these days.

"Why do you have to come in the house drunk every single freaking weekend, Joe?" Angie screamed at her new husband of one year. Her anger surprised Desember, since her mother was such a mild-mannered, go-with-the-flow type. Angie rarely lost her temper, except with Desember from time to time, but generally she was a pushover. Desember lingered a little longer in the shadows of the foyer, concealing her presence as she listened and smiled, proud as her mother took a stand.

"Because," his voice was slightly slurred from the seven double shots of Grey Goose he'd taken to the head earlier, "ain't nothing new. Don't act like you didn't know that I drank every weekend and that I have been doing this long before I met you or married you." He took another shot of liquor, shook his head and added, "And why drink if you don't plan to get drunk?"

Desember's latest stepfather, Joe Livingston, owned a very successful construction business and enjoyed getting bent with his workers on the weekend. It made him feel like one of the guys, even though he was the boss. Joe was usually a nice, kindhearted guy, but liquor would transform him into a monster and make him say horrible things to the people he loved and sometimes cause him to become violent.

Desember never saw him hit her mother, but over the past two weeks, she'd sometimes come home to a broken table, or her mother sweeping up shattered pieces of glass from the floor, or one of Joe's workers fixing something around the house as a result of the aftermath of Joe's weekend extracurricular activities.

"Listen to yourself. Do you hear what you are saying? You seem so ridiculous." Angie could smell the alcohol seeping from her husband's pores. She sniffed loudly. "You're no different from Ned the wino that sleeps by the train tracks, except you got a job." Then she added, "For now anyway."

Desember smiled, proud of her mother's comeback, until she heard a noise that sounded like a firecracker exploding, startling the hell out of her.

Angie fell to the sofa, clutching the side of her fair-skinned face, which now bore a red mark from Joe slapping the cowboy shit out of her. Desember dropped her bag and soda on the table and stepped out into the open.

Joe looked at Desember with malice. The two locked eyes. It was no secret that neither of them liked the other. Desember would have sent his ass packing long ago if she could, but it wasn't her decision. This was one of the main reasons that when her boyfriend, Fame, asked her to move in with him, she couldn't move her things out of the house fast enough. But since their breakup two weeks ago, she was back at home living in the man's house and hated that she had to be there under his roof abiding by his rules.

The feeling was mutual. From the first time Joe had met the girl he thought she had too much mouth, and was too outspoken for any eighteen-year-old girl or for any female, for that matter. He preferred his women to be more passive and submissive, like Angie.

"W-w-whad," he stumbled over the word as he took a sip from an open bottle of Heineken that was sitting on the table. "Whad the fuck do you-uughh . . ."

He was interrupted by a swift and painful knee to the groin, which caused the Heineken bottle to slip out of his hand. Before he could recover, a shiny switchblade jumped out of its handle and settled at the crook of his neck.

Desember spoke slowly and clearly, leaving no room for any misunderstanding: "If you ever put your dick beaters on my mother again, I'll kill you." Her eyes never left his. "This is your first and last warning, you bitch-ass nigga."

Even before she opened her mouth to speak, her hands and dark slitted eyes had already told Joe all he needed to know: that although she was only eighteen years old, she was serious and there was no denying—she was dangerous.

Desember broke her knife down as quickly as she had pulled it out, the tone in her voice sharper than the blade she'd just put away. "It's no threat, it's a promise." Her eyes never left his.

She never blinked as she watched Joe fix his collar. He

turned his back on Desember, looked Angie up and down, then staggered out the door with a crushed ego—and crushed nuts.

After a few moments, Angie broke the silence between her and her only child. "You didn't have to emasculate the man, Desember," she said, her face still showing his red handprint. "You need to stay the hell out of grown folks' business," Angie said to her daughter before running out the door after her man.

"You're welcome, Mom," Desember sarcastically hissed at Angie's back. Desember hated the fact that her mother was, and always had been, dependent on a man. That was one of the reasons she hustled as hard as she did; she didn't want to end up living that way. Desember shook her head and sat down to enjoy her sandwich. Just then Usher and Alicia Keys's "My Boo" ringtone sounded from the phone in her pocket. She knew exactly who was on the other end of the jack and it sent a tingling feeling throughout her entire body as she hit the green button to answer.

"What's up, Fame?" Fame and Desember had been together for three months now, although it seemed like years. They complemented each other like A-1 steak sauce and a New York strip, and she was happy for the diversion from her home situation.

"Let's go to the movies," he said. "That joint with your girl Beyoncé jumps off tonight." He acted as if he didn't know that she was still mad at him.

"You talking 'bout *Dreamgirls.*" It was a statement, not a question. And Fame wasn't feeling the flick one bit, but she knew the man like a well-read magazine, and she also knew the nigga was crazy in love with Beyoncé like millions of other men were with Jay-Z's wife.

"Yeah, that's the one. You wanna roll?"

"Pick me up at my mother's house," she said before ending the call. Honestly she didn't care where they went as long as it was away from Angie and Joe's house.

She had twenty minutes to change. She put on a micro-mini denim skirt that showed off her well-toned legs and ass that boys couldn't keep their eyes off of. She then brushed her three-hundred-dollar weave and added some lip gloss that complemented her flawless chocolate skin.

Exactly twenty minutes later Fame called again. "I'm outside baby, waiting in the car. You ready?"

"Yeah, I'm ready. I'm coming out now," she said right after she heard someone coming in the front door. By the sound of the footsteps, she knew it was her mother returning.

The second she got in Fame's car he greeted her, this time with a long kiss. "I missed you, baby."

His mouth tasted like watermelon Jolly Ranchers. He had a fresh haircut and his waves, which he brushed his hair religiously to maintain, were tight and shiny. His freckles and youthful smile made him appear much younger than his actual nineteen years.

"I miss you too," she said, then her phone rang.

"Where are you going?" It was her mother.

"The same place you went . . . with my man." Desember looked at Fame.

"Dee, you know that he's no good for you."

"You're one to talk," she shot back. "And yours is good for you?" She rolled her eyes. How many times had she heard this song from her mother, who seemed to have one set of rules for Desember and another set for herself?

"We are speaking about two different things," Angie insisted. "And you know it."

"Well, like mother like daughter. If loving *my man* is wrong, oh well, the hell with being right."

"Desember, that boy is trouble. One day you'll learn and it's going to bite you in the ass . . . and when it does don't say I didn't try to warn you."

"I'll deal with that day when it comes, Mother dear. Anyways, gotta go."

$ $ $

The movie theater was jam-packed for the *Dreamgirls* opening night. Fame and Desember took two seats in the very last row, caring more about ducking the eyes of the other patrons than actually watching the show. The chemistry between the two of them was magnetic, and it wasn't long before the darkness and temptation overtook them.

Minutes into the movie Desember reached over, unzipped Fame's jeans and slipped her hand inside, searching with deft, manicured fingernails.

"Need some help?" Fame whispered as he ran his hand up her thigh under her short jean skirt.

"I got it covered, but if I run into any trouble, you'll be the first I let know." After a second or two, Desember had a firm grip on what she'd been searching for.

"I heard that," he said in a cross between a sigh and a moan as he leaned back in the cushioned chair, content to let her fingers do whatever they wanted as long as they kept doing it.

Desember's hand, still slick from the buttery popcorn, glided up and down his hardness. He jerked, trying to fight against the will of his body. The hand job was feeling so good he could no longer focus on his attempt to return the gesture.

"Whatsda matter, big boy? Need some help?" she teased, knowing he was almost at ecstasy.

Despite the darkness, Fame could sense the seductive half smile spread across her face. "Nah, baby," he said in between tense breaths. "I don't need no help, but I've seen enough of this flick. Let's get the fuck outta here before we get caught."

"Don't let me find out you running," she teased, still holding on to his nightstick.

"Oh, you best believe I'm running, all right. But I'm not running away, I'm running toward it. A man can't live on foreplay alone." He could see the movie anytime. In fact he had copped a clear bootleg copy over a week ago, hoping to see it with her. Besides, he hadn't made love to Desember—or anyone else, for that matter—since their breakup.

"Lead the way, big boy, I'm right behind you." She took his hand as they both got up, and after a few "excuse us's" and "pardon me's," they were out of the crowded movie theater and in the parking lot.

Fame held her hand and used his other hand to pull out his keys from his front pocket, then chirped the alarm and lock to his 2007, souped-up Impala.

They drove ten minutes to a low-traffic stretch of the road just off the expressway in silence, except for the sounds coming from the new Jeezy CD. They pulled off the road onto the grass alongside a row of trees.

Desember pushed a button, reclining her seat all the way back and pulled up her skirt. "Turnabout is fair play," she purred.

"Say no more." Fame's tongue made a dive so skilled into her goodness, Olympic judges would have scored him a perfect ten.

Desember was the only person he'd ever gone down on, and over the past three months of their relationship, he had mastered the carnal science.

"Oh shit!" Desember enjoyed every second of it, bucking her hips, giving him all the access he needed in the small space the car allowed.

Fame cupped her butt cheeks with his hands so she couldn't squirm away—not that she wanted to—and lapped at her sweetness until she damn near broke loose, releasing a river of juices. But it didn't end there.

They switched positions and Fame leaned back in the passenger seat, Desember straddling him. She rode his muscle like an equestrian pro trying to break an untamed beast. Every time she dropped her hips, he thrust deeper into her middle, and the louder she moaned.

"That's it, baby!" Fame cried out this time. "Ride that ma'fucking horse." He could feel the pressure building up, his nuts tighter than a pocket full of money in a pair of skinny jeans and ready to explode.

Desember felt it also, and she increased her rhythm. Then after five or six quick up-and-downs, she raised her hips, pausing at the tip, just enough to make him beg her to finish him off. And she did, slithering down his pole until he lost his load . . . and part of his mind. He was still trying to catch his breath when he slipped out of her warm pleasure spot. "That shit was the bomb, boo," he gasped after a long exhale.

She laughed. "Nothing like make-up sex, huh, baby? Plus I missed you so much. I really did." She kissed him.

"You been watching them porn movies when I'm not around?" he teased, kissing her forehead.

It was hard to believe that only two weeks ago they had been at each other's throats—literally—in a fight that not only landed them both in jail but with restraining orders to stay a hundred feet away from each other. But there was nothing on the face of the Earth—no court papers, prison bars, distance, person, place or thing—that could keep them apart from each other, because the truth of the matter was they were chained together at the heart.

Her and Fame's altercations were nothing at all like Angie and Joe's, Desember thought to herself. The difference between her and Angie was that Desember was nobody's punching bag or whipping girl; she gave as hard as she took, and since she and Fame became a couple they may have had heated arguments but it had only gotten physical once. And at the end of the day they truly loved each other. If it's true that for every action there is an equal but opposite reaction then their relationship was testimony to the rule. In their minds, they fought hard because they loved even harder.

"Fuck, naw, I ain't been watching no damn porn, nigga," she shot back with a playful hit. "How about you get yo' mind out the gutter for once and do something useful with yo'self? Try gettin' a towel out of the trunk or something."

"Bet. I gotta hit my seats anyway. You got 'em all wet with that waterfall pussy of yours," he joked, slapping her on the backside before sliding from under her and out the passenger door.

Once outside the car, Fame pulled his jeans up, buttoned them and zipped and fastened them before heading to the rear of the Impala.

It was ink black on the unlit road except for the moon and stars, and rare headlights from a passing motorist. That was why he picked that particular spot: it was quiet, private and dark, and the perfect place to make love under the full moonlight. But to be honest, as hard as Desember had gotten his dick in the movie, he'd been a hot minute from being willing to bust a nut on aisle seven in Wal-Mart.

He hit the lock button on his key ring to pop the trunk; it clicked, then the lid slowly ascended, dim yellow light shining on its contents. Nothing was out of place and even the carpet in the trunk was showroom clean. He always kept fresh towels in the trunk of his car for wiping it down after he got it washed. He worshipped that car like it was his deity.

The plastic crate he kept his clean towels in was sitting where he had left it—in the back right corner of the trunk. He checked the bottom of the crate, underneath the clean, soft, Downy-smelling towels, to make sure his pistol was still in place. The cold, hard cylinder of the barrel gave him comfort. His oldest brother, Felix, once told him that it's better to get caught with it (by the police) than without it (by the enemy) and ever since then there was a better chance of catching Fame in the street without his pants than without his burner.

He grabbed the top towel from the crate and headed toward the front of the Impala.

He heard a vibrating hum from a motorbike approaching from the westbound lane, and his instincts compelled him to look over his shoulder. The one-eyed machine was a ways off, but the roar of the strong high-booster engine was getting louder as it ate up the tarred pavement. It was a little cold to be riding but Fame envied the rider anyway. He had a deep passion for motorcycles, but had yet to purchase one of his own.

This summer, he thought, *I'ma get me one.* He nodded with an envious smile on his mug as the biker closed the final twenty or so yards between them, trying to figure out what kind of motorcycle it was, when the bike backfired . . . five times.

Pop! Pop! Pop! Pop! Pop!

Or maybe not . . .

They were gunshots.

Before he could react, Fame caught the first slug in the shoulder, spinning him 180 degrees. The second bullet missed him, instead ripping a middle-sized hole through the tail end of the whip that he religiously praised.

$ $ $

Startled by the first shot, Desember reacted with her gut instinct and reached for Fame's pistol. After the second slug went into the backseat, she fell to the floor of the car, desperately feeling under the seat for the piece of cold steel that was usually there, but felt nothing. She thought of where else it could be. She knew that Fame wasn't carrying it on his body when he got out of the car, and prayed that by the grace of God he had taken it out of the trunk when he'd gone for the towel. Still unsure of what was going on, she had no other option but to duck her head under the dashboard. The third, fourth and fifth bullets slammed into Fame's side, stomach and back. He collapsed by the car, the side-view mirror revealing his surprised eyes as he lay motionless while the motorcycle and its rider sped off into the dead of night.

Desember bailed out of the car the second she felt the coast was clear and yelled out, "FAMMMME!!!!"

She prayed that he was okay, but once she made it to the driver's side of the car where he'd gone down and found him curled in a fetal position with blood gushing out of his wounds and mouth, she feared that her prayers might be in vain.

"Noooo!" she cried out. "Don't die . . . You can't die . . . I won't let you!" she screamed, dropping to her knees beside the man she loved with all her young heart. She had to pull it together for Fame. *I gotta get him some help. Where's my phone? Dammit! What did I do with the fucking phone? Calm down, Desember. You can't help if you're panicking.* She rose and hurried back inside the car and grabbed her cell phone, frantically dialing 911 before remembering that she had turned it off earlier.

She punched the button to repower the phone and waited an agonizing six seconds—which felt to her like six hours—before it finally turned on.

"What's your emergency?"

"I need an ambulance," she screamed at the nonchalant-sounding voice. "My man has been shot, and I think he's dying!"

Minutes later an ambulance pulled up. The doors located on the rear of the vehicle sprang open, red lights still screaming emergency. Two young EMTs jumped from the ambulance with the efficient speed and ability of the trained and familiar. Together they moved a collapsible gurney from the truck to the ground and gently but efficiently rushed Fame to the hospital.

Desember held Fame's hand. She hadn't released it since she made the 911 call. The truth of the matter was that her love for him ran so deep, she felt that if he was dying she was too. When they were there on the nearly deserted road waiting for help, Fame fought for breath to speak, and she could hear the gurgling of blood in his throat. Fame had managed to say, "I . . . love . . . you . . . D."

Trying to be strong with tears in her eyes, she held it together. "I know you do, baby. But right now try to save your energy. We gonna need all the strength in both of us to get through this. We gonna make it, baby."

Fame was in bad shape, and Desember wasn't quite as sure as she sounded. But she wouldn't give up, and neither would Fame.

At the hospital, two oversized glass doors slid open as they approached, allowing entry into the emergency room. The senior ambulance medic had already called in the situation on the way to the ER: trauma patient, black male, between the ages of eighteen and twenty-five, multiple gunshot wounds, critical condition. They assumed that the slug that entered from the back had clipped Fame's lung, which could prove to be fatal.

Two nurses met them in the ER. It had only taken the emergency vehicle six minutes to arrive at the scene, and another seven to get to the hospital. The technicans were relieved that they had done their job getting their patient to the care he needed. Now it was up to the hands of a skilled surgeon, God and Fame's will to live.

"We'll take 'im from here," the brown heavyset nurse said to the techs. The nurse standing by her side, Mildred, was a white older lady with short dark hair. Mildred's eyes quickly assessed the situation before settling on the clasped hands: one a young woman's and the other a young man's, both stained with blood, holding onto each other for dear life. "You've done all you can do," she said, "but you're going to have to let go now."

Desember looked up into Nurse Mildred's bright, but slightly tired, blue eyes and saw a woman with compassion to her plight, but with a job to do. Reluctantly, she pried her hand away and said, "I love you, Fame. You know I do."

The nurses and doctors whisked Fame away to the trauma room. "We're going to need you to fill out a few papers, ma'am." Desember hadn't seen the nurse walk up. This one was tall, wearing a colorful yellow and purple smock. "Are you related to the patient?"

"Yes, I'm his wife," Desember said confidently. Though they were not legally married, in her heart they were. Marriage was nothing but a piece of paper and in the real world it didn't mean shit. The love they shared meant everything; she was his partner in life, and if it came down to it, in death too. They had been living together and fully committed to each other for the past three months. In their eyes the feelings they shared for each other ran deeper than most couples' who had been together for years. They were down for each other unconditionally.

Nurse Mildred looked at Desember. "This is Nurse Shelia, and she's going to take you to a cubicle and ask you a series of questions, mostly about his medical history, allergies, etc." She gave Desember a reassuring squeeze on the shoulder. "I will check on you later," she said.

Desember went with the other nurse and answered her questions to the best of her ability, until she was distracted by a bunch of ruckus going on down the hall.

"There that bitch go right there!" Fame's sister, Faith, shouted, pointing at Desember so that there was no mistake about whom she was speaking.

Desember knew that all hell was about to break loose, because Fame's family was first-class ghetto. This was one of those times she wished she weren't an only child, but still she'd go toe to toe with his sister or his brothers if she had to.

The nurse could see the tenseness in Desember's face. "Everything going to be okay?"

"I don't know. Those are his family members and they can be a mess."

Nurse Shelia responded, "Nothing's going to happen."

"Well, like I said, I don't know what to expect from these fools. So, if anything goes down," she grabbed a piece of paper and a pen and jotted down a number, "I need you to call my mother and let her know if they lock me up or something, because I got a feeling this may get out of control."

"I won't let that happen. It won't come down to that," Nurse Shelia assured her.

By that time the police had also arrived, and they came over to Desember as she sat in the booth with the nurse, waiting to question her about the shooting.

Faith got louder to gain the attention of the detectives. "Y'all gon lock that bitch up or not?" she addressed one of the cops, her mother, Francine, by her side. Her brothers, Fabian, Frank and Frazier, took up the rear. "She set 'im up. I know that wicked bitch set 'im up. All you gotta do is check the bitch's fucking police record . . . I know the bitch had something to do with my brother getting shot."

"You must be crazy." Desember got up from her seat. The shit was maddening; being accused of complicity to the assassination attempt on Fame's life was insane.

"She ain't even supposed to be around him no ways!" Faith yelled. "What da fuck she doing around him!"

"It's none of your business what we do together," Desember said. "Hate it or love it, your brother loves me. We love each other."

"Right. And you set him up, beyatch. You can try to sell that love shit to somebody else, 'cause I ain't buying it. He's with you and coincidentally he gets shot."

"Why would you think that Ms. Day is responsible for the shooting of your brother?" the older of the two officers asked Faith.

Fabian spoke instead: "I just got my brother out on bond almost two weeks ago . . ."

"And that bitch was in too," Faith said.

". . . and the judge ordered those two to stay away from each other," Fabian finished.

Frank spoke. "That might be true, but shorty"—he shook his head and waved his hand at Desember—"she ain't got shit to do wit it," he said in a sure tone, but his appearance looked crazy; he had a cigarette behind his ear, and half of his thick long hair was braided while the other half was wild. He had on a jean jacket with no shirt underneath and wore a white gold necklace with a diamond medallion. "I'll bet my life shorty wouldn't cross my brother."

"I just want to know if my son is all right," Francine said to the nurse, the worry in her voice and eyes clearly visible.

"He's in surgery now," the nurse explained. "It's going to be awhile before we know if . . . whether or not he's going to make it. The bullets damaged a vital organ, but he has the best surgeon we've got doing everything possible to keep your son, your brother, alive."

Frazier, three years Fame's senior, looked into Desember's eyes for a sign to indicate that she had something to do with his brother getting shot. He almost agreed with his brother Frank, because all he saw was a young girl, in love and frightened. But that wasn't the same as innocent. If he found out that she had something to do with Fame getting shot, she would have to pay.

Tears crawled to the corners of Faith's eyes. "Let me at that bitch!" she shouted.

Her mother held her back, trying to calm her down, fighting her own tears in the process. "You's a dead bitch. A dead-ass bitch," Faith echoed the threat twisted with anger, pain, hurt. "I promise you, bitch: you dead."

Desember didn't take Faith seriously, because everybody knew that real killers didn't give a heads-up before they moved. She needed to focus on who tried to kill Fame. Or were they both the target? She had too much to deal with, and she didn't need the added burden of Fame's family coming at her.

Officer Lyons's left eyebrow rose about an eighth of an inch, as if his mind was processing information and jotting down mental notes to review later. "Look, I can't let you threaten her like that—or anyone else, for that matter."

"It ain't no threat, it's a promise." Faith said.

"Well, *you* are going to have to keep your *promises* to yourself or *we* are going to have to place you in custody. And under these circumstances, it's not necessary. Everybody is under stress. You should focus your energy on what's important: pulling for your brother to make it."

"Yeah but you need to lock up the motherfucking bitch who did it, instead of eating doughnuts and all that shit! Do yo' fucking job!" Faith screamed, damn near spitting on the man during her outburst.

"We will, but we can't if we're refereeing fights between the people who love him most." He shook his head a moment before continuing. "I understand you're upset," Officer Lyons said to Faith, "but all of your threats and hostility aren't going to help matters any. Everybody needs to calm down; we're in a hospital, not a bar."

"Look, mister, we know where we at, and believe me, we wish we weren't here." Francine leveled her eyes at Officer Lyons, her voice like chips of ice. "It's my son, their brother, on an operating table fighting for his life," she hissed. "We know damn well whcrc in da hell we at. Smells like a got-damn hospital to me."

Officer Lyons nodded to his partner. They had worked together long enough that the younger officer knew what his senior partner wanted. "I'm going to have to ask you all to have a seat in the waiting room for now while my partner and I talk to Ms. Day." Francine and her children reluctantly obeyed the officer's wishes.

Officer Lyons pulled a chair up and asked Desember to take a seat. "I only have a few questions," he said. "Basically routine. I'll try to make it as brief as possible. Okay?"

She nodded her head. "Okay."

"So, uh, how long have you known Mr. Maurauder?"

What does that have to do with someone shooting him? she thought. "I've known Fame just about my entire life," she said. "We went to school together."

"Then you probably know him pretty well, I suppose?"

She nodded to the question. "I suppose."

Officer Lyons was watching her while at the same time trying to appear not to be studying her, but instead thinking about the questions he was asking. "Do you know of anyone who would have a reason to want to kill him?"

Desember knew that if she answered that question honestly it would create more trouble and more questions; trouble and questions better left avoided.

"No," she lied. "I can't think of a single person that would want to see him dead."

He gave her a peculiar look. She wondered if he could sense that she wasn't telling the truth.

"Okay," he said. "How long were you two together today?" He seemed to be going in another direction.

"He picked me up—tonight—from my mother's house. Then we went to the movies."

"What did you see?"

"Dreamgirls."

"Was it any good?" he asked.

"Was what any good?"

"The movie."

"I'm not sure. We left before it was over."

"Oh. Okay. Uh, can you tell me why you were parked on the side of the road? Was there a problem with the car or something?"

She thought about the question and her answer carefully before saying, "No, the car was fine. It was us that was running a little hot, if you must know. We hadn't seen each other in two weeks."

He smiled. "I see," he said. "Can you tell me why, uh, Famis Marauder," he read Fame's full name from some notes, "would be carrying a fully loaded pistol?"

"I didn't know he had a gun," she said, "loaded or otherwise."

Desember was aware that she looked and felt like a mess: blood was on her skirt and T-shirt, her new sneakers were filthy and her head felt like a professional volleyball team had used it in a title game.

Fed up with the senseless Q&A, she asked one of the officers, "Do I have to put up with this shit right now? I'm wearing the blood of the only man I ever loved . . . and I'm exhausted."

Officer Lyons told Desember that she could go home and clean up. "But we're going to have to talk to you again later. Maybe you'll remember something then that you don't now."

Desember replied, "No problem, but I won't be going home. I have to be sure he's okay before I can go." There was no way she could leave while her man's fate was undecided. The police understood.

One of the officers asked Nurse Shelia, "Is there a safe place Ms. Day could wait?"

"I can take her to the private chapel," Shelia said, glad to help. "She can wait there in peace," she added.

I don't know if I'll ever be in peace, Desember thought to herself.

But she followed the nurse to the elevator and then rode up to the sixth floor, then turned down a hallway, past a nurses' station and into a small nondenominational room designed for worship.

"If you need something, just go to the nurses' station and ask them to page me. As soon as we know anything at all, I'll let you know."

"Thank you so much." Desember's voice was so oiled with grief and uncertainty, the words could barely be heard.

"And I've got some sweats in my locker that I can let you borrow. They may be a little big, but they won't fall off of you."

"I really appreciate it." She looked up at the nurse with teary eyes.

"I'll go get them and let you clean up a little. Be back shortly." She was back in a flash as promised and waited for Desember to get changed.

After Nurse Shelia left, Desember plopped down on a wooden pew. *How could things be going so well one moment and then end so badly the next?* she sighed to herself. *This can't be happening.*

But it was.

Desember closed her eyes, her mind on autopilot. Everything from the past three months was a vivid picture, and she could recall it all as if it were yesterday. Everything . . . everything she did with Fame . . . and everything he ever told her about, and Fame ALWAYS told her EVERYTHING!

So she thought.

Three months ago . . .

1.

Hate at First Sight

No one could have seen it coming. If there had been a high school poll about who was most likely *not* to hook up, Desember and Fame would have been the clear winners.

The first time Desember laid eyes on Fame was during recess at Carver Elementary School. She was eight and he was nine. The two instantly took a dislike to each other. She was wearing a yellow and green sundress and a pair of yellow sandals, with matching ribbons in her long pigtails.

She was jumping double Dutch when Fame walked up and called her a black yuppie. Fame was about two inches shorter than her and rail thin.

"What you called me, boy?" she stopped jumping rope to ask.

Fame poked his frail little chest out and repeated himself, "I said, you a black yuppie, that's what."

Desember didn't have any idea what a yuppie was, not to mention a black one, but she didn't think she was one and was willing to fight to prove it. And that's what she did.

First, she kicked Fame in the groin, then commenced to whup up on his lil bony behind. One of the teachers had to pull her off of him. Desember never told that it was Fame who started with her first.

That was just the beginning of their feud. Over the years there were more fights and then as they got older they still managed to make verbal digs at each other whenever possible. But toward the end of their high school careers, everything changed. The animosity gave way to a grudging respect. Fame admired her hustle—Desember had been voted most likely to succeed, best dressed and most likely to be arrested—plus she had filled out nicely. And Desember couldn't help but notice that Fame was now a full five inches taller than her with a swagger to match. Recognizing they were kindred spirits—her mouth more than matched his physical bravado—about a month ago, Fame called Desember, for what she assumed was to cop some weed or something. Desember was in the midst of her day, hustling her numerous products. But he hadn't dialed her up to purchase anything. He wanted a truce, and Fame's version of extending the olive branch was five pounds of exotic and expensive marijuana: Sour Diesel—Cali Kush, which rapper and weed aficionado Snoop Dogg had even endorsed as one of the best.

Over the next month they got to know each other better. She would visit him from time to time at his apartment to blow some trees, or play some Scrabble or Xbox 360 or Wii. They went to the movies, parks, took bike rides and exchanged various gifts; she gave him a few outfits and he gave her a diamond-encrusted heart-shaped pendant. And that was only the beginning.

They had just come from playing laser tag and were sitting in his car in front of her mother's house when Fame asked her: "Move in with me?"

Desember answered with a question of her own: "Why me?"

"Because," he said, looking into her eyes, "I know I can trust you, and I think I may be in love with you." Adding, "Both are rare for me, because I trust only a few and love even fewer."

Desember was feeling Fame as much as he was feeling her, maybe more—if that was possible. And she was ready to get out of the house with her idiot stepfather. She couldn't stand living in the same space.

"If I said yes—and I'm not saying yes yet—when would you want me to move in?"

"Today," he said with a smile. "Or whenever you like?" He obviously didn't want her to feel like he was pressuring her.

"Then, yes, I'm down for it."

Desember went inside the house to get her belongings as Fame sat in the family room watching reruns of *Magnum, P.I.* with Joe, who ignored him after a cursory greeting.

Angie followed Desember into her room. "What are you doing?" she asked as Desember started packing.

"I'm moving out," Desember said while folding a pair of jeans.

"Where?" Angie calmly asked, trying not to turn this into an argument.

"I'm moving in with Fame, Mom," Desember said, never stopping her packing.

"Where are y'all going to live? In a hotel?"

"No, Mom, Fame has his own apartment." Desember grabbed a handful of underclothes out of her lingerie drawer.

"Look, Desember, I really don't think that's a good idea."

"Really, Mom? I thought you'd be happy. This way you and Joe can have your personal space." She gathered some more things out of her chest of drawers. "It's what you want, isn't it? To be rid of me?"

"That's not true, and you know it," Angie denied.

"Mom, admit it: things are going to be so much better for you if I'm not here. You know Joe hates me—and trust me, I can't stand him either."

Angie paused before she spoke because she knew that what Desember was saying was the truth. When her daughter was gone things seem to go a little smoother between her and Joe. When Desember was home, she and Joe fought like cats and dogs over the littlest things. For years Angie had been searching for the perfect father for Desember and when she finally met Joe, he had a lot of things that she wanted in a man, but there was no denying that Joe wasn't interested in being a part of Desember's life.

"You know that you and I are a package deal. If a man can't accept you then he can't have me," Angie declared. But Desember was getting older and not a baby anymore so maybe it was time to let her go, make her own decisions. To help make herself feel better, Angie kept telling herself this was only temporary and her daughter would be back soon.

"Sounds good but that's not how it really is. Honestly, you shouldn't get all teary-eyed about this. We'll still see each other every day. I'm not moving to Europe, just across town," Desember reasoned. "Plus this gives you time to work on your marriage." She grabbed her mother's hands. "I really want you to be happy and I know you and Joe having the house to yourself will help."

"But I don't want my eighteen-year-old daughter going to live with a gangsta."

"Mom, he's not no gangsta. He's a nice guy and he's good to me." Desember let her mother's hands go.

"Desember, the boy is trouble and I don't want you to get caught up in his mess. He comes from a family of crooks. Their last name is Marauder, for Christ's sake."

"That's just a name, Mom. They didn't choose it."

"God gave them that name for a reason. And I'm telling you, those people have done too much bad for it not to come back around to bite 'em, and when it does I don't want you to get caught in the crossfire."

"I won't. Fame would never let anything happen to me. Plus I'm smart enough to keep myself safe."

"I don't think this is a good idea, and I'm begging you not to move out."

"Then, Mother dear, what are the alternatives? If I knew who my real father was, I could live with him."

"Don't go there," Angie warned.

Desember had touched a nerve with her mother. The truth of the matter was that when Angie was pregnant with Desember she had tried to pin fatherhood on several different guys. Her first husband left when Desember was a toddler after he found out Angie was trying to pull a Maury Povich on him. The following year, Angie married a guy named Stan, who loved Desember as if she were his own, but the two weren't married long when the Feds gave him twenty years for tax evasion and running a lucrative numbers operation. After Stan, Angie ran into a rut when it came to romance, until Joe came along six years ago.

Desember wanted to make sure she had Angie's attention. "How come you never told me who my *real* father is? Do you know how it is to grow up not knowing if I have real sisters or brothers? Not having the privilege of ever having nieces and nephews? Or just being Daddy's little girl?"

The tears that Angie fought to keep from escaping her eyes showed that this was a delicate subject for her.

"You've always made sure that I had everything I wanted, except for the one thing I wanted the most: I wanted the truth, Mom."

Before Angie could respond, Desember continued as she threw more of her clothes and personal things in bags. "You've denied me the right to have a relationship with my biological father. Even if he was the DC sniper, I would know why if I found myself in the trunk of the car with a rifle one day," she joked. "If he don't accept me, let me see that with my own eyes. Don't revoke that right from me." Desember dropped her own tears. She put her hand up. "Look, I'm not going to force myself to sit through this emotional roller-coaster ride, because it's not going to stop."

Angie stood with her hands on her hips, not knowing what to say as her daughter continued to pack things in suitcases and shopping bags.

"Fame," D called out, "can you put this stuff in the car for me?"

Joe was so happy to see Desember go that he gave Fame a hand with all her bags.

Before she cut the light off in her room, D looked at her mother and said, "Mom, people say that it's bad when you know things, but you know what? It's really worse when you don't."

She gave her mother a kiss. "I love you and I'll call you tomorrow."

2.

House Rules

Once Desember was settled in and she and Fame had christened the apartment by having sex in every room, they sat in the middle of the living room floor in front of the big flat-screen television watching a reality show. D turned to Fame. "Since we're officially playing house, there are a few house rules that must be put into place if we want this to work."

Fame gave her his attention. "I'm listening."

"First," she said, "no matter what happens throughout the day we can never go to sleep mad."

Fame raised a knowing brow. "I think I read that somewhere."

"Me too, but I like it, and I think we should tag it."

"Okay," Fame agreed, and then asked, "What else?"

"Neither one of us should ever let the sun beat us home."

"Cool." He nodded his head in agreement. "I think I can handle these."

"How about you?"

He looked confused when she tossed the ball into his court. "How about me what?" he asked.

"Do you have any rules you want to implement?"

Fame thought for a second. "Only that we gotta eat dinner at my momma's house every Sunday. It's a family tradition that has been going on as long as I can remember, and since I've been all boo'd up with you, I've missed a few."

"Okay," she said. "I really hope your family likes me." She had never met Fame's folks before but had heard many stories about them—most of them bad.

"They will love you, just like I do. I never took a girl home to meet Ma before, but I'm sure they will love who I love." He leaned in, giving her a hot steamy kiss to punctuate his point.

"Anything else?" she asked seductively. Neither could keep their hands off the other for long. Everything was too new and experimental.

"Well . . . not a rule but more of a . . . precaution."

Desember became confused when he pulled out a big chrome .40-caliber handgun.

"A man like me has a lot to gain, but even more to lose if he gets caught slipping. Everybody knows that the quickest way to get to a man is through the people he loves, especially his woman, so I'm going to show you how to protect yourself with this. Besides, you be dealing with a few shady motherfuckers yo'self."

He emptied it before putting the gun in her hands, showing her how to grip it.

It was big, and heavier than she thought it would be.

"All you have to do is point and shoot," he explained. "All that TV shit where they hold the gun sideways, or close one eye . . . that's all bullshit. Now pull the trigger one time."

She looked at him like maybe that wasn't a good idea.

"Go head. I took the bullets out. You do trust me, don't you?"

She answered by squeezing the trigger like he asked. Click!

"That's it." He continued the lesson. "Now when it's loaded it's going to kick a lil bit. That's call recoil. The more powerful the gun, normally, the more it kicks. That's why you hold it with both hands. That's pretty much it. Whenever you think you need to use one: just point and shoot till you get yo' desired result."

Holding the gun gave Desember a rush of power that she hadn't expected to feel. Later she released the pent-up feeling under the sheets before they called it a night.

3.

Knocked

Desember was a natural born hustler. There wasn't anything she wouldn't sell—well, except for her body and her loyalty. She got her start at age nine, selling icebergs to kids in the neighborhood because she didn't want to grow up and be at the mercy of a man, like her mother was. Over the years the products changed: clothes, pills, term papers, but not her natural mentality for the grind. It was no secret: the girl was a mobile store, and everybody knew that Desember always had something that was in demand in the trunk of her car. Some days she had so much stuff that she had to rent a U-Haul to make her rounds.

With a team of boosters that she treated like family, and numerous other plugs aquired over time, Desember was never without product, legal or illegal.

Nobody quite understood where the girl got her hustle. Clearly she did not get it from her mother. In fact, some would say that she wanted to be nothing like her mother, who was always depending on a man, wanting to be rescued.

Today, Desember roamed the aisles of the Recalls discount store with a trained eye, looking for items she could buy low and sell high. The outside looked like a barn but it was actually the best-hidden secret in all of North Carolina. It was a discount store that sold some of the best name brands and hard-to-find items for next to nothing. The three hours it took for her to drive there was well worth the trip, and she usually took the ride once a week to look for things she could quickly resell on the street for a profit. This week they had some Michael Kors bags for $29.99, which she knew she could get $100 to $150 for easily. They also had some perfumes and colognes on sale for $7.99 that went for $59.99 retail. She knew she could sell them for at least $25.00. Plus she was due to pick up a shipment from one of her favorite and best suppliers.

Until she and Fame became an item, D's favorite pastime was acquiring things other people wanted or needed and selling them for a profit. She felt like a kid in a room full of chocolate and gumdrops as she filled her cart with bargains and steals. This was going to be a good week; she had just moved in with Fame, Recalls had plenty of good merchandise, and her favorite booster would have some nice items for her in a few hours. Things were going better than average.

Desember's phone had rung on three separate occasions while bargain shopping; she had not bothered to answer it. If it wasn't Fame's ring tone, what else or who else could be more important than what she was doing at that very moment? The fourth time, she took a look and noticed that all the calls had come from the same number. A number she wasn't familiar with, but something told her to answer it anyway.

"Hello."

"Hey, girl. I been trying to call you. Thank God you answered." The voice was low and slightly tight.

It was Kim, her favorite booster and best supplier. Desember got excited because she knew Kim was ready to deliver some other hot stuff—hot meaning straight out of the department store into Desember's trunk and into the homes of her faithful customers. Just like anything else, since Desember was a faithful buyer and bought from Kim in bulk, Kim sold the stuff to her for next to nothing.

"I saw the strange number on my phone," Desember said, "but I was busy and didn't know who it was. What's—?"

"Girl, I need your help," Kim said quickly. "I'm locked up."

"Shit, Kim. Whad da fuck?" Desember was shocked. Kim had to be one of the top boosters on the East Coast. "What happened?" Desember asked, then realized that the what, when and why information wasn't important right now. "Never mind that." She could find out what happened later. "What jail are you in? And how much is your bail?" she asked instead. "Now don't worry about a thing. You know yo' girl gotcha, chica."

Desember took down the information from Kim, then dialed a bondsman who was one of her customers. She always looked out for him, just in case something like this happened. After working out the particulars with the bondsman, she hit Kim's mother up on the phone.

"Hi, how ya doing, Ms. Taylor?" Before Kim's mother could answer, she introduced herself. "This is Desember, a good friend of your daughter."

The phone went quiet for a second before the slow-talking lady spoke.

"I just got a call from her." She took a deep breath. "I don't know why this girl does this to me. You know I had that girl when I was forty-five and she knows this ain't good for my heart," Ms. Taylor said.

"I know," Desember agreed, wanting to get back to the topic at hand.

"I just got off the phone with her myself," Ms. Taylor, dragging the conversation along, said. "She told me you would probably be calling but I hadn't quite caught your name."

"It's Desember," she stated clearly, and shifted back into business mode, "Well, anyway, I've already got e'rything worked out with the bail bondsman. All I have to do now is shoot by your place and give you the money. He's going to meet you at the jail so you can sign for her."

Even though Desember loved Kim and they had gotten a lot of money together, she knew better than to sign on the dotted line for anybody, because if they didn't go to court then that was her ass, and she had enough of her own bullshit to have to deal with someone else's.

"That's fine," Ms. Taylor said obligingly. "How long before you get here? I'm getting dressed now. Been in most of the day—ya know, ever since I came in from the doctor."

After Ms. Taylor ran off the address and a few other non-pertinent pieces of personal information, Desember punched the street address into her navigational system and said, "I'll be there by six-twenty."

"Six-twenty?" Ms. Taylor questioned.

"Yes, ma'am, I'm coming from a ways away, but don't worry, I'll be there."

Scarface said in the movie: "All I have in this world is my balls and my word." Desember didn't have balls to worry about, but she never broke her word.

4.

A One-Track Mind

Clark Station Projects was an open-air market for drugs, prostitution, soliciting, stolen goods, violence and then some. Like most poverty-stricken neighborhoods, life wasn't as promising or *promised.*

Desember parked her 2004 red Altima in the visitors' parking space with two things on her agenda. First, she wanted to recoup the money she'd just given Ms. Taylor for Kim's bail. Second, she wanted to pay a visit to her best friend, Kayla, who had been calling the infamous projects home for one month shy of a year now. Since Kayla's eighteenth birthday, the day she told her mother she was pregnant. In return, Kayla had received an ultimatum: "Get an abortion or find somewhere else to live."

Kayla chose the latter and Desember had helped her furnish her apartment and supplied all of the baby clothes and necessities. Since the baby's daddy was MIA, D was both godmother and father to little Kaylisa.

Desember was looking for Midget Man, one of her best customers. She knew she could make her money off of him alone. As she searched the scene for him, she was interrupted by a voice.

"Hey, girl," Vanessa greeted Desember as she pulled up and got out of the car. "You got some mo of dem Deréon jeans like the ones you sold Keeva last week?"

Vanessa was a well-developed brown-skinned chick that sold pussy throughout the projects. She had a regular clientele of white boys that came through, and Keeva, light-skinned with green contacts, was her only competition.

"Girl." Desember smiled and got in hustle mode. "You ain't no last week type of bitch, and I'm not gon even try to carry you like one. I got some newer, hotter shit for yo ass."

One of the first lessons a good hustler must learn (and Desember was definitely good at what she did) was that if she didn't have what a potential customer needed or wanted, she made them think they needed or wanted what she had.

Vanessa's face lit up. "That's why I fucks wit yo' ass, girl," Vanessa said, grinning. "I might buy two pair if you got 'em in size eleven."

Now Desember was the one grinning. "I just so happen to have two pairs of elevens that I was holding for you anyway." Desember was kicking game.

After breaking the ice with Vanessa, business wasn't booming, but it was fair, and she hadn't crossed paths with Midget Man yet. D had made five or six more sales when a dude walked up wearing a pair of tight-ass skinny leg True Religion jeans with a matching shirt and fleece jacket, and a silver medallion swinging on a forty-inch silver chain.

He stopped in front of Desember. "Whad up, shawty?" She gave the dude a hard look because she didn't know him. "I heard you got the new Gortex boots like the ones the nigguh Gucci Mane wo in 'is last video."

She wasn't feeling the dude's swagger at all, but that had nothing to do with business—especially if his money was green. If cats wanted to let Jim Jones and them dudes dictate how they dressed, who was she to object?

"Yeah, I got 'em." She nodded. "I got one pair left in a size ten and a half."

"That's me all day, shawty," said Silver Chain. "What they hitting for?"

"Well, they cost like two fifty in the store, but I'm doing 'em for one ten."

"I've got seventy-five dollars right now," Silver Chain propositioned, obviously feeling himself. Desember detested an arrogant-for-no-reason-at-all nigga.

"And you still got it," she told him, not taking any shorts.

"Bitch, I know you ain't going to let no funky-ass thirty-five dollars stop you from getting money."

No, he didn't.

"First of all"—she waved her finger—"whoever you think you is, I make money, money don't make me. And second"—she moved her neck around a bit—"I damn sho ain't gon let yo' petty ass stop me from getting mines either. I don't tell you what to sell those lil tiny-ass crack rocks for, do I?"

"Bitch, don't get yoself fucked up out dis piece!" he exclaimed in a voice loud enough to get the attention of a few people in earshot.

"Who gon fuck me up, nigga?" she came back, looking him dead in his face, and he was holding his tough-guy stare beat for beat.

"Bitch, don't play with me," he barked after the slight. "Stay in a bitch's place and you'll live longer."

She didn't flinch or back down. "Nigga, I wouldn't waste my time with a petty-ass nigga no way," she returned fire. A few people started to sneak peeks in their direction, and as the sun was going down, the daytime crew was being replaced by the night crew, who hung out in pjs.

"Fuck you, bitch. Stupid-ass bitch. Fuck you, you nowhere-ass bitch."

She cut him off before he could could continue with his bitch campaign. "I ain't going to be too many mo of yo' bitches, and it takes two to fuck, so you need to pay more attention to your position before you fuck around and be the one assed out." Then, twisting her neck, she added, "Nigga."

Silver Chain looked like he was about to flip or blow a good gasket or something.

Fame had warned her that her mouth was too raw for some people, but dude had started it. She shrugged her shoulders, didn't budge; she maintained her position with her hand on her hip. Akimbo style.

He turned his back and walked away. Desember went on to help her next customer. Meanwhile Silver Chain quietly pulled out a chrome nine and pointed it at her pride and joy, squeezing the trigger three times. Just as he let off the final shot a patrol car turned into the project's parking lot. Silver Chain didn't wait around to answer any questions from the law.

The police cruiser made its way in the direction of the origin of the gunfire. Desember stood by her car in shock as she stared at the three nickel-sized holes in the passenger side of her Altima, which she had grinded for all by herself.

Though she was mad as hell, when the police asked her what had happened, she told them she didn't know. She'd seen the building that Silver Chain had run into, and she even saw him peep out the window twice.

She cut her eyes at the window when the police weren't paying any attention and gave him the middle finger and mouthed, "Fuck you, nigga."

Trust and believe it wasn't fear that stopped her from handing Silver Chain over to the po-po; it was her belief, or rather what she didn't believe in: she wasn't a snitch-ass bitch, and she couldn't stand the got-damn cops!

$ $ $

Over the next couple of hours D laid low in Kayla's apartment. As she was about to leave, she saw Silver Chain coming out the cut. Desember took off running at full speed. And had cameras been rolling, Nike would have paid her a pretty penny for the performance she put on: she was more entertaining than Michael Jordan and LeBron James combined when her Air Jordan-adorned feet rose off the ground. Before Silver Chain knew it Desember had caught him from the back with both of her hands wrapped around his neck in a choke hold, causing him to lose his balance and fall to the ground.

Once she took him down, she was in complete control. As mad as a demon on steroids, adrenaline made her feel as if she had superhuman strength. She rammed Jackass's head into the concrete over and over again, and she didn't stop until she realized he was unconscious. "I bet you won't mess with nobody else's car, you bitch-ass nigga."

Realizing that he had gone unconscious scared her so bad that she got up and left him there. As she made her way to her car and out of the projects, she heard someone scream, "Call 911!"

Once she was out of the pjs she pulled over to the side of the road, rolled a fat blunt and smiled. Though she'd have to file an insurance claim and pay a deductible, in her eyes the debt had already been paid. She felt like the ass-whipping that she had put on Silver Chain was payment enough. Indeed, she had really taken the cost of the damages out of his ass.

When Silver Chain woke up the next morning at a girlfriend's apartment, still in the projects, he was thankful to still be on the bricks. If the chick had pointed out to the police where he was, he would have been a goner. He was already a convicted felon, on probation with ten years over his head—not to mention the gun charge alone would have given him five years mandatory in prison. Despite being a little bruised up, he smiled.

As he walked toward his whip, the smile vanished. What the fuck is this? All four of the brand-new tires on his truck were sliced. There was a note under his windshield wiper: *Life's a bitch, then we die!*

5.

Meet the Fam

It was a picture-perfect Sunday afternoon in Flowerville, North Carolina: the sky was a cloudless, brilliant blue, and children were playing carefree, as only the youth know how, enjoying the last day of the weekend in the clement 65-degree surroundings while mature red, orange and brown leaves clung to the only home they'd known, some falling from those very same branches onto green lawns, like uninvited guests to a Labor Day cookout.

The driveway was full, so Fame pulled over to the curb in front of his mother's modest three-bedroom house. It was several decades old, like most of the others in the neighborhood, but well maintained. His mother, Francine, made sure of it; she took great pride in her home.

Desember sat next to Fame in the car, uncharacteristically

nervous. Fame gave her a pat on the thigh. "It's going to be fine, boo," he said. "They shit and wipe they ass the same as you."

Actually the Marauders were one of the most, if not *the most*, infamous families in the small county of Flowerville. And they were as thick as thieves: if one got into a fight, they all fought. They had a reputation for anything illegal: murder, drugs, assaults, extortions—always finding themselves on the wrong side of the law.

The patriarch of the family was Felix Sr., who was on his nineteenth year of doing a 25-to-life sentence for killing a man with a baseball bat.

The story was that at the age of twelve, Felix Marauder, Jr. was already a little menace, on his way to being a young terror. One day he got caught blowing up one of his neighbors' mailboxes with a cherry bomb. It just happened that this particular neighbor played on a rival softball team against little Felix's dad, and they couldn't stand each other.

When the guy found out who Felix's father was, he made the mistake of telling Felix Jr. that his daddy was a no 'count bully full of hot air—Felix Sr. showed him a bully. According to the court documents the neighbor was more than sixty pounds bigger and a full six inches taller than Felix Sr. But the extra height and weight did him no good at the hands of the meaner mercenary, Felix Sr.

Once the prosecutors showed the jury pictures of the dead man's head, split open like a melon, they dismissed any thoughts of letting Big Felix slip through the cracks with a self-defense plea.

After the incident, Felix Jr. decided he wanted to follow in his daddy's bootprints. He got what he wanted. Six years later the same prosecutor who convicted his father worked a case against him, and in the end, Felix was sentenced to fifteen years in the same maximum-security prison. They became cell mates—repping Flowerville and the family name.

"I don't want to look like an outsider trying to get in where I may not be welcome. I know how close y'all are." She knew how much family meant to Fame but was more concerned with how much Fame meant to her. She loved him so much and didn't want his family to be the deciding factor in her being his wifey for real.

Fame ran his tongue across his bottom lip. "You just as much my family now as my blood brothers and sisters," he assured her. "And don't forget it." Then he leaned in and gave her a kiss. "Now let's go in."

As soon as they walked through the door a girl who looked too much like Fame not to be related jumped up from the couch. They both had the same pecan-colored skin with cinnamon freckles all over their faces.

"This is my sister, Faith . . . this is my girl, Desember."

Faith didn't even acknowledge Desember, who was about to speak when Faith turned her back and made her way over to the kitchen. "Ma . . . Fame got a girl wit 'im."

Desember wondered how she would act if she had a brother and he brought a girl home. *Damn, I would have at least spoken and tried to make her feel comfortable,* Desember thought. Just then Fame's mother, Francine, came flying into the front room, hands wet, clutching a dish towel. She was about 5'6" and apparently the donor of the skin tone and patch of cinnamon dustings her kids sported.

"That's my mother," Fame stated the obvious.

"I'm Francine, but people call me Fran," Fame's mother

said in a matter-of-fact manner—not too cold, but not too warm either.

With her hand extended, D said, "My name is Desember. It's nice to have finally met you."

Francine offered a hesitant handshake. "What type of name is that?"

"It's the one that my mother gave me," Desember said in the same cheerful tone, but it was a little harder to deliver. "It's spelled with an *s*, not a *c*."

"Oh . . ." was all Francine said, then, "Nice, I guess."

These people are not making this easy, but hey, women never do, Desember thought, but she didn't waver.

"Yo two knuckleheaded brothers are in the den playin' video games with they ol' asses. Fabian . . . Frazier."

"Where Frank at?"

"Taking a shit as always." Then Francine called out, "Come in here and speak to your brother and his friend."

The two brothers came lumbering from another room. One was about six foot, the other about 5'10", the same skin and freckles as the rest of the family.

"That's Fabian," Fame said, nodding to the taller one. "And that's my other older brother, Frazier. And this . . ." now talking to his brothers, "this is my girl, Desember."

Fabian and Frazier both studied Desember, from her crisp new Air Jordans, up to her well-shaped thick legs and heart-shaped butt, which her skinny jeans made hard to miss, and settled in her intoxicating cognac eyes and slightly naughty smile.

"Damn, lil bro," Fabian spoke up first, "I see you traded the chicken dinner for a bona-fide winner," giving Fame a good-natured rub on the head.

"What you see in that dude?" Frazier teased, looking directly at Desember before shooting his eyes over to Fame, then back to her.

If possible Desember's eyes got even brighter, body language exuding the core of its normal confidence. "That's easy." She beamed. Her pearly whites shone in contrast to her dark chocolate skin. "I see everything in Fame."

Fame tried not to blush but failed.

"Ma," Fame tried to divert some of the attention from him, "are you having a card game tonight?"

"Boy, I sell drinks and cut a card game e'ry Friday, Saturday and Sundays, don't I? Or you done got so caught up in Ms. Thang you plumb forgot how yo' momma be doing hers?"

Fame knew his mother was just taking shots at him because he'd pulled a no-show on the last few Sunday dinners, but that didn't give her a right to disrespect his girl. He also knew that if he didn't straighten it now, the possibility was very strong that it would spiral out of control.

"Her name is Desember, Ma . . . and I haven't forgotten anything or anybody. Believe that. I just want everybody to treat Desember like family. She's a part of me—that makes us one big happy unit. Ride or die!"

No matter if Francine and his sister never accepted her, Desember had never felt so proud of the way Fame stepped up to the plate for her.

"Excuse me, Ms. . . . I mean, Desember. Don't mind me; I just like having a little fun," Francine said, although D wasn't convinced. "Let's sit down and grab a bite to eat, and then y'all can help me get this place ready for this evening. You play tonk, Desember . . . with an *s*?"

"No, ma'am."

"Nothing to it," Francine said, smiling. "You'll learn. You may drop a couple of dollars in the process, but you'll learn, I tell you."

"Somebody call Frank so we can eat."

Faith went and banged on the bathroom door. "Frank, get off the toilet and come on, you holding us all up."

Frazier yelled, "People hungry, man."

"You heard dat Frank got jumped the other day, man?" Frazier asked Fame.

"Naw, I ain't hear," Fame said.

"Man, we gonna let him tell us dat shit over grub," Fabian interjected.

They had a little small talk around the table as Francine set the food out. Then the bathroom door popped open.

"What the fuck that crazy bitch doing in my house?" were the first words that came out of Frank's mouth.

He was the only sibling who didn't inherit his mother's freckles and pecan skin tone. He must have gotten his looks from Felix Sr. Frank was rocking a bandanna on his head; but she could see that he was trying to conceal a bandage on his forehead.

Everybody turned to him, dumbfounded. Faith spoke up, "First, this is your new sister-in-law."

"She ain't no fucking sister of nothing of mine," Frank said, then immediately changed his tone, "Naw, this my buddy right here," as he apparently thought about how he couldn't let on that she was the attacker responsible for the bandage on his head.

Frank extended his hand to Desember.

She felt as though she'd seen a ghost. "Oh, my GOD, that's the guy that shot up my car," Desember said in a low voice to Fame, finally really getting a good look at him.

"You shot my girl's car up?"

"Hell, yeah, that bitch mouth is too reckless," Frank defended his actions.

"Not sweet little Desember, with an *s* not a *c*," Francine interjected; she didn't want her boys to spoil the Sunday dinner as they had been known to do.

"Yeah, that bitch is crazy."

"She ain't no bitch!" Fame stood up.

"She ain't no lady either the way she was telling me to kiss her ass and how she would fuck me in the ass."

"Whoa!" Frazier intervened.

"She jumped me. Her and three other niggas," Frank lied.

"Frank, you shot the girl's car up?" Faith couldn't believe it.

"Man, this shit is crazy," Fabian said with a smile. "And you let a girl beat you up," he ragged on his brother.

"The bitch is the fucking devil, but one thing for sure: she's one of us." Frank smiled. "I ain't mad at cha."

"For a minute, I thought you won't gon fit in with us," Francine chimed in, now that the drama was subsiding.

"Frank, you gon pay for her car," Fame said.

"Yeah, he gon pay for the car," Frazier interjected. "He shot it up."

"Fair enough, and I know a shop for her to take it to." Frank extended his hand to Desember. "Truce? You got my respect. I don't wanna be your enemy."

Desember smiled, meeting Frank's hand with her own. Her heart was now out of her panties. At first she thought it was going to get ugly.

Over dinner, Frank and Desember each gave their version of the prior events. Desember felt that everyone in Fame's family warmed up to her, except Faith.

I can chop my food up, Desember thought, *with the daggers this chick is shooting at me with her eyes. Family or no family, I'm going to have to keep my eye on this bitch!*

6.

Showtime

Fame slowly tried to slip out of Desember's arms and the bed without awakening her. But Desember had been wide awake for a while, thinking of how content she was laying up with her boo.

"I was hoping to lie around in bed a little longer," she said, obviously surprising him. "Where are you off to this morning?" she asked, not ready to release his warm, hard body.

Fame took a sip from a glass of water on his nightstand. "I thought you were still asleep, not playing possum."

"Possums play dead. I always feel alive around you," she said, propping a couple of pillows against the headboard to sit up better. "You didn't answer my question, though." Fame never lied to her, but he would sometimes avoid a question to conceal the truth.

He sat naked at the side of the bed. "I got some business to take care of today."

"You can't spare a few more minutes?" She put her hand in his lap and flashed that mischievous smile of hers. "I'll make it worth your while."

After a tug or two, parts of him wanted to say the hell with it and jump back underneath the big down comforter, but his more intelligent half resisted the lure. The clock on the nightstand read 11:13 A.M. Desember was still trying to work her magic on her man. The *decision* was rock hard.

"I may be a fool for it," he said, finally making up his mind, "but I've gotta go. It's going to take at least an hour to get to where I need to be," he explained before giving her a soft kiss on the lips. "Rain check?" he suggested.

She pulled the covers off to reveal her naked body and lay on her side in what she thought was a sexy, enticing position. "A man can't live off work alone," she tried one more time, even knowing it would do no good; his mind was made up.

"Nor will all play put food on the table." He wanted so badly to try to catch a few more snuggles with his boo, but his dedication to his hustle wouldn't allow him to.

Fame got up and stretched, his manhood pointing north, and headed into the shower.

By the time he was dressed Desember had cooked him two healthy-sized bacon, egg and cheese sandwiches.

"You can eat one now," she said when he walked into the kitchen, "and take the other one with you–if you like." She was wearing a pair of boy shorts and a fitted wifebeater.

Hc thanked her and then wrapped both sandwiches in Reynolds Wrap and hurried out the house before he changed his mind about leaving.

$ $ $

Fame was a different kind of hustler—some people did the wrong thing for the right reason, and were looked upon as criminals, some did the right thing for the wrong reason, and were looked upon as heroes. Fame fell under neither of these categories: he robbed because he was good at it. He chose flashy drug dealers because, in his mind, they deserved to be robbed if they were caught slipping. Better him than the police.

He sat in his car, up the block from his target. He knew from staking out the house for the past week and listening to people run their mouth that the chump who lived there was called Big Ty. He migrated to Charlotte from the Big Apple (or Rotten Apple, depending on who you ask) about four or five years ago and quickly added to the already growing drug trade in the otherwise welcoming area.

Word on the street was that Big Ty had the best, unlimited crystallized Peruvian flake the area had ever seen. Drought, famine or recession—dude always had work. And to keep the Feds off, supposedly, he never sold more than an ounce at a time, although the jury was still out on whether the "no weight" policy was a precaution or just another way to increase his profit.

Fame checked the time on his dashboard clock. It was 1:55 P.M. His phone rang. Against his better judgment, he answered, in case it was important.

"Hey, baby," he said into the Bluetooth.

"Hey, you."

"What's going on? Everything okay?"

"Yeah, everything is cool. I was just thinking of you, that's all."

"Can you do me a favor?" he asked, his eyes glued to the house and his surroundings.

"Do a chicken lay eggs?"

"I'll take that as a yes."

"Then you would be taking it the right way. What's up?"

Looking down at the remaining breakfast sandwich, he told her, "I want you to make dinner for me." Desember wasn't the best cook but she was getting better and he appreciated the effort she put in.

"You promise you gonna be home for dinner?" she asked.

"Fa 'certain, baby. I'll be there naked with bells on by six."

She chuckled. "A'ight, what you want me to cook, baby?"

"I want turkey wings and some yellow rice."

"Okay, baby, what else?"

"A nice bottle of champagne," he requested, although neither was old enough to drink.

"Okay, what else?" she asked. "Anything else I can do for you?"

"I want you to find something nice and sexy to wear for your man."

"What else?"

"Oh, make some mashed potatoes too."

"Okay, baby, what else?"

"And I will bring the stacks of money when I come home."

"Then we don't need anything else."

"A'ight, I got to get off of here and focus so I can get the job done."

"You always get the job done," she said in a sexy tone.

Fame ended the call with Desember and took his eyes from the ranch-style brick house to steal another look at the time. Big Ty's girl left the house every day at 2:20, and this day was no different. *Right on schedule. Probably going to work.* But Fame didn't know for sure. However, he did know that she was always away from the house for hours. He waited an extra thirty-five minutes just in case she might have forgotten something and returned. If things got ugly, he thought, it was always better to leave one dead body behind, rather than two. But then again, if it came down to it, dead was dead.

Showtime!

Getting out of the car, Fame took one last good look around, went to his trunk and removed a small black and gray toolbox and a clipboard. He placed a cable company hat on his head and headed toward Big Ty's residence. He wore a blue work uniform and black soft-bottom boots and appeared to be an average everyday worker trying to make a living.

Once on the porch, he could hear the faint sound of music on the other side of the door, and though he couldn't make out which cut it was, he was sure it was something by Jay-Z. Fame pressed the doorbell.

"Who is it?" someone asked from the other side.

"Cable man." Fame had disconnected the wire that sent the main feed to Big Ty's system earlier that morning. He knew it would take at least twenty-four hours before the real cable company would respond. That type of attention to detail is what kept him on point when it came to his job. He had uniforms and equipment from all the major companies, as well as access to their dispatch systems.

"That's what's up, son," Ty said, opening the door. "I didn't expect you guys to send someone so quick."

"Dispatcher said that there would be a lady expecting me. She was adamant that we needed to get out here sooner rather than later."

"Yeah, that's my bitch and shit. She can't live without that Lifetime shit, but she gone to work and forgot to tell me that y'all was coming. Glad you got here, though, son."

Fame hated when niggas from up top hit him with that "son" shit, but now wasn't the time to reveal his personal hang-ups. Not right now, anyway.

Big Ty stepped to the side so that Fame could enter.

That was the best part to Fame. When he robbed cats, it was always at least 50 percent con and the rest robbery, sometimes more con than stickup. By the time the victim knew he was being beguiled, it was too late.

"So," Fame said, "exactly what's going on with the cable?"

"The shit won't show a picture," Big Ty complained.

"So you're not getting any channels at all?"

"None," Big Ty told him. "All I'm getting is a few hundred channels of snow, son." New York accent in full bloom.

"How many different sets do you have hooked up to your system?"

"Well." Big Ty pointed toward a fifty-inch flat screen mounted on the wall. "There's this one. Then there's three more in the bedrooms. Oh, and the one in the game room. That's in the basement."

"That's five in all." Fame quickly tabulated as he pretended to jot something down on the clipboard. "Do you mind showing me where they are? I need to check the feed to each unit before running a circuit test on the main line," he bullshitted.

What he wanted to do was make sure no one else was inside the house. He hated surprises, and an unknown guest was the last thing he needed; it could cost him everything . . . most of all, his life.

"Not a problem, son." Big Ty led the way, his Levi's hanging off his butt, his crack showing. He was a big guy, standing about 6'2", over 250 pounds. He was built solid and was much bigger than Fame, but Fame knew size didn't mean a damn thing. After all, the nickel nine millimeter that Fame was packing had taken down even bigger guys, and he was sure that Ty wouldn't dare to challenge it.

"Yo, you from out here, son?" Ty asked.

Wanting to hurry up and get this over with, Fame nodded at Ty though technically he wasn't from that part of the state. He knew better than to shit where he slept.

Big Ty took Fame into the three bedrooms, and Fame, playing his part to the hilt, turned on each television, touching the cables running from the back of each with a current detector he'd gotten from Home Depot.

Nobody was upstairs but them. Fame said, "Okay, you say there's a fifth one around here somewhere?" The round schoolboy glasses he wore sat crooked on his face. The perfect nerd look.

"In the basement, son." Big Ty stole a glance at his oversized diamond watch. "How long do you think this is going to take?" he added.

"After the basement," Fame said, "it's pretty much a wrap, son."

"Word," Big Ty said with more enthusiasm in his voice than before. "It's this way." Fame followed him down the hallway, through the kitchen and down a flight of carpeted steps.

The bottom level was one giant room, covering the length of the house. A professional-sized pool table with crimson felt was off to the right. To its left was a six-chair poker table. The opposite side of the floor space was set up like a den, with a couch, love seat, recliner, two red end tables with glass tops, and a 62-inch Sony television as the focal point.

"Nice lil setup you got yourself here," Fame complimented the man.

"Yeah, I know," Big Ty said, with great pride and confidence in his voice, "A man has to have his own little sanctuary, even in his own home."

"That's what's up." Fame groped down into the toolbox he was carrying, came up with the nickel nine and a pair of matching cuffs. Big Ty's eyes grew to twice their size. Fame threw the metal cuffs to Big Ty and said in a firm tone, "Put these on. Talk only when spoken to. Say nothing stupid and maybe you'll live to enjoy it again. Oh." He pointed the Llama between Big Ty's eyes, just above his nose. "Don't ever call me 'son.' I hate that dumb shit."

After being restrained and threatened, Big Ty did the right thing. Neither the money nor the cocaine was worth his life.

"The money and the work are in a safe upstairs, in the office closet. Take it . . . take it all. Just don't kill me." He didn't sound nearly as confident or arrogant as before. His voice was a pitch or two higher and the corners of his eyes showed fear and were wet from the tears beginning to form. "Please just don't kill me."

"I'm a man of my word; do as I say and you'll live." The tears didn't evoke any sympathy from Fame, but they did bring on a smile as he asked a final question: "What's the combination to the safe?"

When it was all over Big Ty was ashamed that he had pissed his briefs, but was happy to be alive. He would never forget the incident or the man who pulled it off.

7.

Just the 2 of Us

Fame loved when a well-thought-out plan came together. The hit on Big Ty was sweeter than expected. He'd scored over two hundred thousand and ten keys of 80 percent pure coke.

As Fame had promised, he was in the crib before six, waiting for Desember to finish hooking up dinner. He admired her toned legs and petite frame as she stood over the stove cooking in her birthday suit.

He walked up behind her. "You are busted." He kissed her on the neck.

"Busted?" she asked, feeling his manhood growing against her bare butt.

"I'm calling *Cheaters* on you."

She turned to face him and shot him a look. "You been drinking?"

"Naw, but you're busted."

She had no idea what she was busted for.

"That Crock-Pot filled with the wonderful smell isn't ours. It's yo' momma's."

Desember almost choked she laughed so hard. "You got me. Damn, you good, Detective Famous."

The truth of the matter was that Desember wasn't a good cook, and she knew it. Yet Fame never complained and tried all of her cooking and ate it until the last bite was off his plate, no matter how horrible it was.

At the dinner table, Desember asked Fame to say the blessing. He looked unsure for a moment and then the look melted away. After clearing his throat, he closed his eyes and began:

"God, we ask that you may bless this food, and if you see fit, protect us from our friends, for we don't always know their intentions for us. I'll take care of our enemies, for theirs are more obvious." He opened his eyes. "Amen. Now let's eat."

Desember watched as Fame enjoyed the tender turkey wings that Angie had done her thing to. The woman may not have been perfect, but she cooked divinely. They were interrupted by the Lil Wayne ringtone.

Desember gave Fame a chastising look. "No phones at the dinner table, darling!"

"I know, baby, but it's my brother."

Desember knew there was no point in arguing with him, especially when it came to his family.

She couldn't tell much by the one-sided conversation. Fame mostly listened, only asking, "Where at?" and "How long?"

Once he hung up, he turned toward Desember and said, "I gotta go do something for Frank."

"When?" she asked, and then made up her own answer to the question. "Sometime tomorrow, right?"

"Nah, it gotta be done now."

"So you leaving out right now?" she protested.

"I got to."

"You don't have to."

He nodded. "Yeah I do. It's important."

"Baby, I stopped doing what I was doing so that I could come home and be Mrs. Domestic and now you gonna eat and run. That shit ain't right."

"I know, but you act like I planned it—something important just came up, that's all."

Desember didn't hide the fact that she was pissed. She raised her voice. "More important than spending time with me?"

"You know nothing is more important than spending time with you. You know that." He attempted to kiss her, but she turned away.

"Don't try to play me."

"What, you mean don't kiss you?"

"You probably leaving me here because Frank is introducing you to some bitch since he can't stand me. He doesn't want us together no way."

"Baby, that ain't true. Frank fucks with you and you know it," he tried rationalizing with her.

"Fuck that." She raised her voice again. "I'm not gonna keep taking the backseat to your family. I don't do that shit to you. You move me in here and barely stay home, now you gonna leave me by myself to go deal with Frank's ass. You know he ain't nothing but trouble."

"Actually, it ain't even Frank's shit. Fabian asked that Frank go deal with it and he can't, so I'm gonna handle it. It's in and out. Just picking up some money, that's it."

"Just money?" she questioned, still skeptical, but wavering somewhat.

He nodded. "Yeah, just money."

"Then cool," she said, walking out of the kitchen and into the bedroom.

Fame sat in the front room gathering his thoughts before he left. He hated when they argued—and besides, he needed to have a clear head when he went into the trenches.

Before he knew it, Desember was back. She had thrown on a BeBe sweat suit and sneakers to match. "A'ight, I'm ready."

"D, where you going?" he asked, out of curiosity.

"What you mean, where I'm going?" She shot him a look like he was asking her an absurd question. "I'm going with you."

"No, you not. You can't go with me."

"Why, if it's going to be so simple, quick, in and out?"

"Because where I'm going is no place for a lady." Fame tried to put down his foot without raising his voice. He never yelled at Desember. He'd done enough of that when they were kids.

"Well, I'm going." She folded her arms and gazed into his eyes.

He returned her hard stare with one of his own. "No, you are not."

$ $ $

Fame pulled up in front of the beige house that needed to be power-washed to get its factory color back. The trees and the greenery that surrounded the house made it hard to see past the gates when he put the car in park.

They sat at the curb. "Remember our deal," he said to Desember, shooting her a look that said he meant business, "stay in the car."

"I remember." Desember sighed deeply. "You only told me three or four times already."

Before he got out of the car, he said, "Good. Then we shouldn't have any misunderstandings or problems." She watched as he walked into the mini forest until she lost sight of him.

Her phone rang. It was Kristin, her half fake sister or whatever one would call her. Kristin was Daryl's daughter. Daryl was the first guy that her mother said was her father.

Daryl was the only father Desember knew up until she was three years old. He loved her like only a father could love his daughter, until the whispers behind his back—and sometimes to his face—finally got to him. No one in his family believed Desember belonged to him; her dark skin and cognac-colored eyes were so different from his light complexion and gray eyes.

To put the rumors to rest, nine days after Desember's third birthday, Daryl took a paternity test. It was a week before it was returned, shattering reality as he knew it. She wasn't his child.

He loved Desember, still to this day, but the betrayal by Angie was too much to bear. He could have managed to get past the infidelity, but not the deception. Six months later, Darryl moved on, ending his marriage—or lie—of four years. Since then, he tried not to treat Desember any different, but you can't fake being a daddy with a heart filled with hate and mistrust of that child's mother.

D's first instinct was to ignore the phone call, but since she had nothing to do but sit in the car and wait for Fame, she answered.

"Hey, Kris,"

"Hi, Sissy."

That Sissy shit really annoys the hell out of me. She asked, "What you up to?"

"Nothing much. I was calling you because Chelle said that you told somebody that you ain't any kin to us." Chelle was Kristin's younger sister. Kristin was fourteen, Chelle thirteen.

I ain't, she thought, but said, "That ain't true; I said I was an only child."

"Why do you say that?" Kristin sounded confused.

"Because I'm my mother's only child." Desember knew that Kristin loved her, and she didn't want to hurt the girl, but the truth of the matter was that *she* was hurting. Kristin and Chelle knew who their father was, but Desember might never have the luxury that other kids took for granted. It wasn't fair . . . but life wasn't fair.

"Yeah, but that doesn't make you an only child, and you shouldn't feel like that."

"Well, I do."

"How come?"

"Because y'all all got the same momma, and y'all momma isn't as welcoming to me, and I don't really fault her."

After some small talk about how Kristin and Chelle were doing in school, Desember realized almost ten minutes had gone by and Fame hadn't returned. It shouldn't have taken him this long to get in and back out.

"Look, Kris, I love you and the whole nine, but I gotta go. I need to make a call. Hit me tomorrow, I got some nice jeans in your size." She ended the conversation abruptly and called Fame's phone, but he didn't pick up. Desember waited five minutes and dialed his phone again—still no answer. Somewhere in the pit of her stomach she felt something wasn't right.

Desember had promised that she would remain in the car, but some promises were meant to be broken.

She was determined to get to the bottom of things, so she opened the car door, shut it softly and crept through the mini forest. When she got to the back of the house, she saw a few doghouses and chains, but no dogs in sight. It looked like someone was using the area to train dogs to fight. Her mind drifted to the NFL star Michael Vick's cruelty to animals scandal. The fact that the person who owned the house was into such a vicious sport made her even more suspicious that something wasn't right. This wasn't the time for her mind to drift, though.

From a distance, but close enough to clearly see, Desember peered through one of the windows of the house. She wasn't prepared for what she saw.

There were two dead bodies sprawled across what was probably the dining room floor. WOW! she thought, *This shit is real.* One had a hole in the center of his forehead, a macabre third eye looking out for him in Hell. The other looked like he had taken traumatic shots to the face, and Desember couldn't tell who he was.

He was dressed all in black, the same as Fame.

God, no!

Fame couldn't be dead. She hadn't even heard any shots go off. If she hadn't been on the phone with Kristin, she thought, maybe she would have heard something. Maybe Fame wouldn't be stretched out on the floor in his own blood.

Then Fame walked into the room carrying a black briefcase and a gun with a silencer attached to the barrel. She looked up to the Heavens. *Alive. Thank God.*

That's when a loud sound frightened Desember, causing her to jerk around.

It was only a barking dog.

But in the dark, she couldn't tell where it was. Although, judging by the vicious sound of the animal, if it were free to attack, she would've known it already. Just to be on the safe side, however, she continued to scan for the dog . . . until someone put a hand on her shoulder.

Spinning on her heels, knife out, she managed to catch the dude across his upper body.

"What the fuck?" It was Fame. "I thought you agreed to stay in the car." The knife had glided straight through his leather jacket, but missed him—barely.

"I was afraid something might have happened to you," she said, her heart pounding in her rib cage. "When you took so long to come back, I got worried."

Fame still had the gun she'd seen from the window . . . and the briefcase. "Where's the gun I gave you?" he asked.

If I had it, you'd be dead, she thought. Thank God she didn't, and he wasn't. "I don't like carrying it unless I know I'm going to need it. You," she leaned in and spoke quietly, "said this was just a money pickup, so I didn't bring it."

"You never know when you're going to need a gun, until you need it," he warned. "Afterward will be too late. Let's get da fuck outta here."

In the car D decided not to mention what she saw through the window, and instead asked, "Sooo, what happened in there?"

"Nothing happened. I got what I came for."

A few minutes of silence passed before she spoke again. "I wasn't afraid."

"Fear can sometimes save your life," he told her, keeping his eyes on the road ahead of them.

"Maybe so, but I'd rather be confronted by a ski-mask-wearing goon swinging a warm gun than a bitch hiding behind an insincere smile and a concealed knife ready to twist it in my back any day."

Fame smiled at her bravado but remained quiet, allowing her to have the last word. After all, he'd had no intention of laying anyone down when he left home tonight, but the pickup turned out to be a trap set to kill his brother. Luckily he peeped it when he did or he would have been the one lying on that dirty floor.

He also knew that Desember had seen more than she let on, but that was cool. She had proven time and time again that he could trust her . . . even with his life.

8.

Drop It Like It's Hot

Desember entered the apartment after a long day of working and overheard Fame talking. He had the call on speaker, so she was ear hustling.

"Man, it gotta go down tonight or else you going to have to wait until next month," Tommy said. She recognized his voice.

"I don't have my shit all the way together," Fame told him.

"Man, I'm telling you tonight is the night you gotta do it. The nigga is too cheap to get the security he gon need, so most of what he do have is gonna go to the front end of the club. Getting to him is a piece of cake, and getting the cheese from him is going to be like taking candy from a baby."

"A'ight, I'ma make it happen. Somehow, some way," Fame assured Tommy before hanging up.

Desember greeted Fame with a long kiss.

"So what's good?" she asked Fame while massaging his tense shoulders.

"I'm thinking about a job I gotta do tonight."

"Why can't you postpone it? Do it another day?"

"Because it ain't that easy. The nigga I got on the inside said it's pretty much tonight or never. He's the one that gave me the tip and tonight is the night it gotta happen, but I don't have the help I need."

"I feel ya." Desember paused for a second. "Well, one monkey never stopped no show. We just have to revamp the plan and make it do what it's gonna do."

He turned to look at her. "No *we,* it's me."

"I know you can handle yours," she said, batting her eyes, "but if you need help . . . you know I got yo' back."

$ $ $

Dominique Fuller owned the newest, hottest and hippest strip club in Raleigh. It was both chick- and dude-friendly. The male and female bartenders were attractive, and all were skillfully trained to prepare all the regular intoxicating drinks, along with a plethora of exotic, colorful and frozen ones. Most club owners wanted to skimp on the liquor sold to the patrons to maximize profits, but Dominique was different, because he knew the more intoxicated his customers were, the more money they'd spend on the girls.

The sex business generated billions of dollars a year worldwide and Dominque was cool with his small slice of the pie. But that wasn't the only billion-dollar industry he had his avaricious hands in. Everyone who knew Dominique knew his strip club was established and backed by drug money, although most thought—incorrectly—that he'd given up the drug trade years ago. He was much too greedy and his taste much too exquisite to retire from it, though.

Friday night was Ladies' Night at Dominique's—ladies got in free—and it was packed as usual, but this wasn't any regular Friday night. It was the second of the month, payday for a lot of folks—the military, the government and the drug boys as well.

"Damn, nigga, this line moving slow as a sum-bitch," complained one of the waiting customers as he looked back at the block-long, winding line growing behind him.

Two nice-looking women stepped up to the bouncers when their turn came. At least one of them was fine, the bouncer thought. The other would do, but she wore a little too much makeup for his taste.

"I'm going to have to see your ID," he said to Desember. "You look a lil too young to drink."

"Thanks for the compliment." Desember smiled. "It's in my genes. You oughtta see my mother. Unfortunately, I left my identification at work. I hope that won't be a problem." She batted her false eyelashes.

She did have good *jeans,* the bouncer had to admit. She was wearing a pair of distressed True Religion jeans that clung to her well-shaped apple butt and her thick legs like a coat of wet blue paint. She was rocking a pair of stylish black Ray-Ban glasses, and behind them she had in a set of hazel contacts. On her neck was a big elaborate temporary tattoo of an Egyptian cat. The bouncer paid almost no attention to the tall chick with Desember. She was wearing a silk printed flowy dress, big designer shades and a shoulder-length wavy wig.

"Nah, that's not going to be a problem, ladies." He put pink bands on both their wrists to show the bartender they were of age. "Come on in. Enjoy yourself," he said, mostly to Desember.

Once inside, Desember grinned at Fame. "You don't look half-bad dressed like a girl. You should maybe try it more often, explore your feminine side a little," she joked.

"I got yo' feminine side right here," Fame shot back. "Besides, these Spanx got my nuts jacked the fuck up." He adjusted the tissue paper that was stuffed in his size 34-C bra.

Desember laughed. "Whatever you do, baby, don't hurt the family jewels."

The music in the club was banging. A girl who resembled a young Vanessa Williams with a bigger rear end was working not only the pole but the patrons. If she dropped it any hotter, they were gonna need the fire department on standby. And the excited crowd was cheering her on by the sound of the applause, whistles, shouts—and a flood of paper money carpeting the stage green.

Fame leaned in to Desember's ear so he didn't have to scream to be heard over the racket. "Let's go get a seat somewhere in the back." He wanted to give his eyes a chance to get acclimated to the dim light so he could check out the place and be out of sight at the same time.

As they were walking away, Desember was distracted by the Vanessa Williams look-alike shimmying up the pole like a gymnast. Once at the top, she flipped upside down, spreading her legs in opposite directions, closing them with a scissor motion, then turned upright and slid down the pole, full speed again, slamming her crotch on the platform in a split. The crowd went bananas and Desember stood in amazement, trying to commit the moves to memory. "We not here to take a pole-dancing class, we're here to do a job," Fame reminded her.

Sitting in a corner with Desember, he checked out his surroundings. His pistol was jammed in the Spanx shaper he wore, pressed firmly to the front of his waist by the elasticized material.

Women went to great lengths to be beautiful, he thought; and so would he, to pull off a good lick.

Tommy had informed Fame that near the restrooms in the rear corner of the first floor was a set of double doors that led to the kitchen/storage room. Beyond that was Dominique's office, if what Tommy told him was true. He had no reason to doubt it; Tommy's word was usually on point.

Fame looked at his watch, and, according to a reliable source, Dominique would be in the office at that very moment, counting money. Dominique trusted no one with his paper; word on the street was that he had even put a spy in the club to oversee the bar and door money. All the strippers had to pay 25 percent of their tip money, and if he felt shorted in any way, the culprit would be beaten and banned from the club, maybe worse.

A Young Jeezy cut was playing when a short biracial Asian/black girl climbed on the stage like an untamed, sleek panther. Fame was just about to rise from the table. "I'm gonna go take a closer look."

Before he could get up, though, a waitress wearing a black micro-minidress walked up with two blue drinks on a tray; she set the glasses down on the table. "From the gentleman over there," she said over the music, pointing to an overdressed wannabe pimp in a purple suit.

The purple suit cat raised his own glass when they looked in his direction, as if making some type of long-distance toast. Fame became grim.

This wasn't good. The last thing they needed was an admirer getting in their mix when they accepted the drinks. But by rejecting them, it could cause even more of a scene if purple suit was half the clown he looked to be.

Desember took charge. "Tell dude thanks for the drinks, and I will be sure to get my boyfriend to repay him as soon as he gets finished working the door."

"Will do," the waitress said in an understanding tone, winked, then gracefully shook her ass to the beat as she sashayed away to deliver the message.

"I hope dude don't make me put a hot ball in his ass," Fame said, after the waitress was out of earshot, agitated with the tight Spanx and being hit on and ready to get the job done.

Desember started laughing softly, then a little harder.

"What's funny?" Fame wanted to know, still mad about being hit on by a man. Never mind that he was dressed as a woman. It still felt insulting.

Desember raised an eyebrow and tried to match Fame's tone. "Dude is probably hoping that he could put one in you too, but a different kind of hot ball." Then she cracked up laughing again.

Fame didn't feed into it. "Look, stay focused on the risky business, not the risqué business. We here to work."

"Aye-aye, Captain."

"This is what's up. If I come from the back and don't look at you, wait ten minutes before leaving and meet me at the spot we agreed on."

She nodded. "Cool."

Fame left the table.

When he got to the ladies' restroom, he made a quick scan, then slid through the double doors. The room he entered was large and dark. Off to the right was an oversized wooden door. It was closed. A line of light was shining from underneath it. He pulled the Glock from under his dress and quietly made his way to the source of the light.

Closer now, he heard movement from inside the room.

Dominique was there, just as Tommy had said he would be.

Fame put his hand on the knob and twisted.

It turned.

Dominique looked to the intruder, surprised at first, then his face revealed annoyance as he saw that the intruder was a woman. "BITCH—"

Then he saw the .40-caliber Glock and stopped mid-sentence.

He regrouped. "What the fuck is going on?" There was a little bravado in his voice, as he tried to mask his fear and surprise that somebody was able to get to him.

"Your worst nightmare, chump. But whether you wake up from it or not is definitely up to you." Fame's eyes swayed to the large mahogany desk, the surface full of stacks of money. This was Dominique's cash drop-off spot, until he had the dope money counted and relocated to a safer spot. Only he knew the location of the latter.

"Are you crazy? You think you can rob me and get away with it?" Dominique's anger mounted. Pellets of sweat formed on his brow.

"You the one that must be crazy if you think I'm not," Fame said calmly. "Dead or alive—on your part—but I'm leaving with the paper."

Dominique looked as if he was waiting for something to happen, like he had the upper hand somehow. Fame was ready to knock the smug look off of his face, when he heard something behind him. He jerked around to see who it was.

"You good, baby. I got this fool." It was Desember, his ace in the hole. She had her gun in the back of what must be one of Dominique's goons. "I saw him come in behind you, but he didn't see me until it was too late," she said.

"Now that e'ryone's here, time to party. Get on the fucking floor now, and maybe you'll be able to get up off of it after I'm done," ordered Fame to the two men.

Dominique and his goon did as they were told. Dominique was a fool sometimes, but he wasn't a damn fool, that's for certain. "Take what you want . . . you got that. Sometimes you gotta accept your loses and live on to fight another day."

"Keep your gun on these two for a second."

While Desember kept the two men honest, Fame snatched a couple of extension cords from the wall and used them to tie both men's hands and feet together.

Everything on the desk was slid into two large plastic trash bags Fame had brought along for the occasion. They made it out a back door with over three hundred thou. It was easier than getting head from a trick with a pocket full of rocks.

$ $ $

They got out like bandits in the night, and once they were home, Fame dumped the contents of the bag on the bed, and Desember counted the take. As she sorted everything to count it, she held up an envelope. "What's this?"

Fame took it out of her hand and examined it. A smile broke

across his face. "This here is the remix," he stated, having realized that it was Dominique's power bill. He figured it was his main residence. Tommy could never find out where Dom lived but knew that wherever the guy laid his head, there was probably more paper to be had.

Desember didn't understand the gold mine she had found, but Fame did. He took her in his arms and they made passionate love on top of the three hundred thousand dollars of stolen money.

Fuck the six-hundred-thread-count sheets.

9.

Clearance Sale

The action was heavy in the Clark Station Projects. The sun was shining but the temperature was still cool. That didn't stop the natural grind of the projects, and Desember was a natural-born hustler taking advantage of all the elements.

She had a small U-Haul truck full of must-go merchandise: king and queen comforter sets, mattresses, ten cases of champagne, iPods, Sony PlayStations, winter coats and clothes for both kids and adults. Kim had hurt the stores with a few well-backed stolen credit cards. Not to mention the E-pills she'd gotten from Fame. It was the third of the month and Christmas was now less than two months away. Money was jumping like corn liquor and nigger jokes at a KKK rally.

Desember had just sold another mattress set and she watched two teenage boys get it off the U-Haul truck while their mother gave instructions on transporting it. Her phone rang; it was Fame.

"What, baby?" She spoke loud to be heard over the commotion.

He ignored the question and asked his own, "Where are you, D?"

"Out here getting paper this first of the month." She had left the house at 8 A.M. and it was now 2:45 in the afternoon. "You know the early bird gets the cake."

"You mean the worm," Fame corrected.

"Fuck the worm, baby," she corrected his correction, "I'm just chasing the cake, boo." She put a finger up, directing the girl who had just walked over to give her a moment, and then got back to Fame. "Where you at?" She tried turning the tables.

"I'm in the crib." She could hear a touch of irritation in his voice. "Where I thought that you would be by now. I'd planned to lay up today, you and me, watch a movie together or something."

"Don't nothing come to you in your sleep but a dream," she shot back. "You know that only a broke bitch should be in the house when the bank is open." Desember was feeling herself. It wasn't even three yet and she had netted over three thousand dollars' profit. She had no intention of going home until everything was gone.

For Desember the hustle was more for the sport than the money, but the paper was a helluva perk. Fame knew her addiction to the grind before they hooked up. He used to call her Energizer Bunny on crack. He just had no idea that his baby girl would choose the thrill of the streets over the thrill he could give her at home.

"Plus, I got something I want to talk to you about," he said.

The girl who was waiting on her to get off the phone mouthed, "Do you have any more of dem Deréon jeans?"

Desember nodded and put her finger up again, telling the girl to wait. "I got a second. What's up, baby?" she asked while looking through a huge black plastic shopping bag.

He said, "I'll get at cha later about it, when you can spare more than a second."

"Don't be like that, baby, I'm always all yours. Tell me now. Please?" He loved when she begged. "I got the same jeans that'll fit your daughter," she said with her hand over the mouthpiece of the phone to the girl who was waiting. "She's about a 6x now, right?"

"You dat bitch for knowing that. I just started getting her size last week."

"Okay," Fame said, breaking down, "I was thinking maybe we could go to Vegas next week. Neither of us ever been and it ain't like we hurting for paper. We might as well enjoy it. What you think? Down for a week or so in Sin City?"

"How much for dem both?" the girl asked, referring to the jeans for herself and her daughter.

"Give me fiddy for both."

"What?" asked Fame.

"My bad, baby. I was trying to get this girl what she wanted," she explained, admitting to the distraction. "I'd love to go to Vegas. Sounds divine to me. I'll call my mom and get the number to the travel agent she uses, okay?"

She gave the girl the two pairs of jeans in exchange for the $50. As the girl was walking away, she turned and hollered back, "Oh yeah! Midget Man's girlfriend is up top, so you might want to get word to her. You know she love spending that crazy-ass nigga's money."

"I know that's right," Desember agreed, and had a smile on her face when Fame spoke up.

"Midget Man?" Fame questioned, not wanting to believe that Desember had gone against his wishes. "Don't tell me you in Clark Station."

Desember didn't respond immediately, but her silence was answer enough.

"Didn't I ask you not to fuck around over there?" The accusation was in the form of a question. "That ain't a place for a lady," he continued, "especially no lady of mine."

He was past being upset with her; to say he was highly disappointed would have been an understatement.

"You feel like you can do whatever you want—Ms. Independent—but I ain't trying to roll in that type of relationship, ya hear?"

That was the last thing she did hear before the phone went dead.

Desember tried calling him back over and over, but Fame wouldn't answer. The nigga could be even more stubborn than her when he got mad.

Well, the bell had already been rung; she couldn't take it back—that was impossible. She decided to finish unloading her things, chill out to catch up on gossip and news with her friends, and hopefully Fame would forgive her by the time she got home.

$ $ $

Desember snapped the phone shut again. "Fame can be so damn stubborn sometime. Why won't he just answer the phone?"

Desember was sitting in the front room of Kayla's apartment, on the cream Italian leather love seat, which contrasted beautifully with the strawberry paint job. The interior décor made Kayla's apartment by far the flyest in the project complex; it didn't look like a project inside of her apartment.

Kayla was across from Desember, in a recliner, sitting with her baby girl in her arms, searching for the right words to say to her friend. "Ain't that the pot calling the kettle black?" Kayla pointed out while she rocked little Kaylisa.

"Meaning?" Desember looked offended. Not because of the statement, but the person making the statement.

"Meaning, you are one of the most stubborn people I know," said Kayla. "God only knows, girl, I fucks with you like grits and cheese but you can be a lot to handle sometimes."

Desember gave her friend a look like she'd had one too many shots of liquor, but neither of them was drinking.

"And don't give me that look, like you can't believe I said it. You know it's true."

"It's not," protested Desember. "I'm almost always accommodating."

"Yeah, for your clients, as long as it accommodates you or it guarantees that they coming back." Kayla got up slowly, careful not to wake the baby. She padded barefoot across the pink carpet, which covered the entire apartment, and placed Kaylisa in her playpen, located in the center of the room.

It was out of character for Kayla to go against her, so Desember sat back and waited as Kayla voiced her thoughts.

"You're my best friend since the sandbox in the yard at elementary and I love you like a sister, but let's be honest. . . ."

Desember repositioned herself so that she was sitting at the edge of the love seat. "Okay," she agreed, "let's be honest. I want to hear this."

Kayla sat back down. "I've never met anyone," she said, looking directly at her best friend in the world, "who wanted what she wants, when she wants and where she wants like you."

Desember objected, "That's not—"

"It is true," Kayla cut her off. "But that doesn't make you a bad person," she said. "In fact, that's what makes you who you are."

Desember thought about what she had heard for a second. "So you saying I'm a spoiled-ass control freak?" she asked.

"No, I'm—Well, yes, I am, I guess. But it's only because you know what you want," she added. "I wish I was more like you sometimes. Who'd of thought you and Fame would ever in a million years get together in the first place, the way y'all used to fight like the Hatfields and McCoys?"

"We did use to go at it pretty hard, huh?" She thought back to her and Fame's fights.

"Did y'all? If they were rocking dem reality shows like they do now, y'all two would be filthy rich. That shit was true drama at its finest, girl."

"That ain't no lie," agreed Desember. "Now, we still argue from time to time. You know, just to let 'im know that I'm still that bitch."

"And he must be that nigga," Kayla reminded her. "Because don't get it twisted, you always shined like the star you are, but since Fame made it official, the sun came in second to yo glow some days, girl." Kayla got up again, this time heading to the kitchen. "You want one of these apple wine coolers, girl? My mouth is dry as shit and I need a buzz, I ain't even gonna lie."

"You know they my shit, bitch," Desember accepted, turning in her seat. "Don't act like you forgot who turned you on to them joints."

Kayla grabbed two bottles out of the fridge, gave Desember one, then said, "I'ma put Kaylisa in the back so we can fi'e up a blunt to go with the coolers."

"Yeah, that's right. Her ass too young to be getting fucked up like her mother," Desember joked, tired of being the one under the spotlight.

"Bitch, I barely smoke weed once a month," Kayla shot back, "and when I do, it's with yo ass."

Desember raised an eyebrow in thought. "Okay, you got me there," she said as she pulled a sandwich bag from her Gucci purse. "Hurry up, tho, 'cause dis shit here," holding up the bag, studying it like there was something alive inside, "Fame said this shit right here is that flame, girl!"

"I might not be ready for that shit, then, girl," Kayla said, half-joking, half-serious. "I ain't graduated to the majors yet."

"Me either," Desember admitted. "I guess tonight is draft night, huh?"

Half a blunt and two wine coolers later, both girls were out cold on the sofa and love seat, the other half of the blunt resting in an ashtray on the table.

10.

Slipping

Cedar Woods was the most upscale apartment complex in the city. It had its own indoor swimming pool, clubhouse and 24-hour weight room, plus tennis, handball and basketball courts. Inside, the walls were thick enough to provide extra privacy from neighbors with sensitive hearing to other people's business. The apartments came with every single amenity to make the home more pleasurable. Outside, everything was meticulously taken care of by a well-staffed maintenance crew.

At apartment number 1743-H, a worker tapped on the door. After about fifteen seconds, the man checked his clipboard, confirmed the address, then knocked again, this time a little harder. When he heard someone stir on the other side, he unconsciously wiped away some imaginary dirt from his crisp work uniform. He knew that bad appearances could cost a presenter their job, especially during a recession.

"Who is it?" a gruff voice barked from inside.

"Maintenance," Fame answered, as if lying came naturally. When the door opened, "I'm checking the air-conditioning filters and the batteries in the smoke detectors, sir." After the phone call with Desember, Fame set his mind to take care of some business, and get it off of her for a while.

The man who answered the door was in good shape, tall, dark-skinned, with a clean head and neat-cut goatee. He had a cell phone pressed against his ear and appeared irritated by the interuption to his conversation.

"Hold on a minute," to the person on the phone. Then he asked Fame in a rude tone, "What did you say you wanted?"

"Air filters and smoke detector batteries, need to check them; it'll only take a moment, sir."

The man with the goatee gave him a once-over, then a small nod of acquiescence. "Make it quick," he said, "I gotta few things to do, okay." He was a man used to giving orders.

"Not a problem." Fame slid by the dude and started flipping pages on his clipboard as if he were a coach going over his pregame plan.

In the streets, Goatee went by the name of Carson. If talk on the street was right, he'd been in the drug game for over two decades and had never seen the inside of a jail a day in his life or even a holding pen. Rumor had it that Carson had a family connect from St. Maarten, but Fame listened closely, and there was no trace of a foreign accent in his voice. *But that means nothing,* Fame thought to himself. If a Chinese baby grew up in France, among a French household, the child would speak perfect French. Humans mimic what they hear.

Cedar Woods was one of many places that Carson held down. He supposedly also had other houses in North Carolina, New

York, California and on some island. Perhaps St. Maarten—who knew? All Fame was sure of was that the nigga was strapped. Fame had gotten lucky obtaining the whereabouts to this one.

Fame's homeboy Pockets, who worked at the car wash, was always on the lookout for somebody to hit up. He'd seen the address and registration to Carson's Jaguar when he stopped to get it detailed at Carpool. Fame watched the apartment for two months before he finally spotted Carson, and could pin him down to somewhat of a pattern.

Now the man was watching Fame closely. "Look here, I'm going to have to call you back," he said into the phone before ringing off and clipping it to the waist of his jeans.

Fame swapped the batteries in the alarm positioned in the ceiling of the hallway, and then he did the same thing to the one in the kitchen. Afterward, he took a look at the ventilation duct, the one that sucked the dirty air out, and checked the filter.

"Do you know the last time this was changed?" Fame asked.

Carson shook his head, not much of a talker apparently.

"I need to go to the truck and get one," Fame explained. He walked back toward the front door to block any possible retreat from Carson, then Fame reached under his blue work pants and removed the people mover. "But first," he said, "I'm gonna have to get a few things up off of you."

The minute Carson spotted the Glock, his eyes sparked a look. "I should have known better. My wallet is in my back pocket." He pulled it out and slowly handed it to Fame.

The billfold was crammed with big-faced Franklins. That would have been a decent score for a small-time dude, but Fame knew better. There were bigger fish to be had in these here waters. He tossed the wallet to the floor. "This ain't no joke, nigga. I want the real money."

Carson offered some unsolicited advice. "Your greed may be your undoing."

Fame answered by cracking him upside the temple with the gun, drawing blood. "Let me worry about my undoing! You just do what the fuck you're told," he snarled.

Carson attempted to walk away. "What you think you're doing?" Fame snapped.

"You come for da money, right? It's in the back," Carson replied, in a matter-of-fact kind of way.

Fame followed, with his gun pointed at Carson's back, to the bedroom at the end of the hall. The furniture in the room was huge, a giant mahogany king-sized bed, matching dresser, with a huge mirror that took up an entire wall, a couple of night tables and a file cabinet that was the same finish as the furniture.

Carson went to the cabinet, twisted a small key into the slot on top and then opened the upper drawer. It contained at least fifty manila envelopes filled with stacked hundreds, ten thousand a stack, five in each envelope. The contents of one had spilled out when Carson tossed the packages on the bed.

Jackpot. Fame was amazed at the good fortune he'd put himself in position to cake up off Carson.

But he could barely believe his eyes when Carson opened the second drawer and started tossing more stuffed manila envelopes on the bed, where he'd piled the others.

Fame was so busy calculating the numbers, with his back turned to the bedroom door, that he failed to register the mistake, or exactly how much danger he was in, until it was too late.

Out of nowhere he got bashed over the head from behind with a big-ass picture frame. He had seen it on the wall in the hall earlier, a picture of Bob Marley with an oversized spliff hanging from his mouth.

Before Fame could regain his composure, Carson knocked the gun from his grip and had him in some type of choke hold.

Fame twisted, ducked and grabbed at Carson's arm, but none of it worked. The grip was vise tight. If he didn't get out of the hold quickly, he would lose consciousness. His gun was now on the other side of the room, out of reach. Carson was screaming in his ear, "Yo try to kill me, fuck boy, huh? Yo don't know who yo fuck wit," he angrily said, unmasking his native tongue.

Fame wasn't sure where the person who had hit him with the picture had run off to, but he was thankful he wasn't also whaling on him. Almost about to black out, he lurched as hard as he could, backward, knocking Carson into the dresser mirror. He cracked his head, glass shattered and a large jagged shard cut into the back of his neck.

Carson's grip loosened.

Fame elbowed him with all his might; the solo flex. It didn't take long before he broke free of the hold. With only a fraction of a second to make a quick choice: go for the gun on the opposite side of the room or the door, which was closer. The decision was hard for him, because he never left without what he came for—but Fame chose the door.

Carson must have gotten to the gun, because Fame heard erratic gunshots as he ran down the steps three at a time and fell into the passenger side of the waiting car. Pockets jammed the already running car into gear, stepped on the gas, and they bailed out.

"What the fuck happened?" Pockets asked once they were out of the immediate threat of danger. Fame hadn't spoken since he'd gotten in the car looking half dead, trying to catch his breath.

His neck was bruised, and his lungs were burning from lack of oxygen. "I need something to drink." The words came out froggish. His eyes were rimmed with red. They finally pulled over at a gas station to get a bottle of water. It was the best water he had ever tasted in his entire young life.

Fame looked at Pockets and held up Carson's billfold, which he had scooped up in mid-stride from the floor of the apartment while running for his life, and said, "Shit, my nigga, dinner on the rude boy?"

They shared a small chuckle after pulling safely into the lot of a familiar restaurant.

11.

The Showdown at Sunup

Fame had a box of Cap'n Crunch, a giant plastic Tupperware bowl and a half-gallon jug of milk sitting on the kitchen table as Desember quietly opened the door of the apartment.

"Where you been?" asked Fame between mouthfuls of his favorite cereal.

It was 8:23 and Desember had just came home, being the first of the two to break her own rule by letting the sun beat her in.

The potent bush that she and Kayla had smoked in conjunction with the wine coolers they had drunk had put both of them on their asses, out for the count. She woke up on Kayla's couch at about 7:30 A.M. with a dry mouth and a cramp in her neck.

"If you hada answered your phone," she said dryly, "you woulda known where I was last night." In her mind, he had no right to question her; he was the one who'd been funky last night.

Fame dropped his spoon into the bowl, handle completely submerging into the milk. He looked like he was ready to blow up but amazingly he kept his composure when he said, "If you had been home where you belonged, there wouldna been no reason to use a phone."

He scanned her body for the first time. Her clothes were wrinkled from sleeping in them and her hair was sort of jacked up because she hadn't wrapped it.

"We can talk about who was wrong or right later," she said, walking away. "But right now I need a shower and something to eat."

Feeling disrespected, even more so by Desember turning her back to him, Fame leapt from his chair.

"Don't fucking turn your back to me in my house!" he yelled. "What? You trying to go wash some nigguh off you before you come near me?" he accused her. "You think I'm a fucking clown or something?" He grabbed her shoulder.

"Not until you started talking like one," she barked back. "Now I'm not too sure who you are." She could see the hurt and anger in his eyes and face, but Desember didn't give a damn at that point. She wanted to hurt him the way he had cut her with the remark about sleeping around. "A real man," she continued, "wouldn't have to ask where his wifey spent the—"

Before he realized what he had done, Fame had slapped the only woman he'd ever loved. He instantly regretted his actions. "I'm sorry, I didn't mean . . ."

Desember was stunned momentarily. He hadn't put his hands on her in anger since they were in middle school.

Before Fame could get his apology out, she was clawing at his face and eyes like a wild animal, a woman trying to protect herself.

Fame knew he was wrong, but now all he could do was try to defend himself from her punching, scratching and kicking.

They were making so much noise that one of the neighbors, probably old lady Connie, called the police. Fame was never so happy to see the law in his life, because when it came to Desember, he was a lover, not a fighter.

By the laws of North Carolina, once the police are called and have to intervene during a domestic dispute, someone has to leave the house, and if there's violence involved, someone has to take a ride in the squad car.

In this case, after the police saw the damage done to Fame (mostly from Carson's house) and the light mark on Desember's face from the slap, there was only one thing to do. Neither wanted the other to go and both admitted that it was their fault, but the police still hauled them both away.

$ $ $

The cells were six feet by nine feet: green walls, a steel rack—painted the same color as the walls—posing as a bed, and a stainless steel toilet/sink combination thingamajig. There was a huge light on the wall over the toilet, and a vent that pushed cold air in even though it was the early winter.

There were only four of them in the entire miniature police precinct. For the past forty-five minutes, Desember had been housed in the cell closest to the front, Fame in the one next to hers. The town drunk occupied the one farthest to the back. He would be there six to eight hours, sleeping off his latest attempt at killing himself by way of Cold Duck.

Deputy Jock was fifty-four years old, but could still wear his military uniform from when he had joined the army at eighteen. His black low-cut shoes were spit shined and his brown deputy digs were cardboard crisp. "The magistrate wants to see you at the same time," he said, pulling them both.

The magistrate was sitting in her closet-sized office: a wooden desk, a file cabinet and a picture of Ground Zero from when the Twin Towers were destroyed in New York.

"How are you two doing today?" asked Magistrate Dobbson. She was 44 years young, her blond hair wrestling with gray and her figure reflecting a penchant for good cooking. After both Fame and Desember said they were okay, she lifted a paper from her cluttered desk. "Famis Maurauder and Desember Day," she read from the warrant. "You two like to beat up on each other, huh?"

Desember tried to explain first how they had just had a misunderstanding and nothing like this had happened before, Fame agreeing to whatever she said. They only wanted a bond and to get out of there.

"Well," Magistrate Dobbson said, gazing at them both to try to see if they were being honest with her, "from the looks of it, things got pretty ugly. Domestic violence is no small matter. Something I've never tolerated, and I don't intend to start now." She gave them a lecture.

Fame looked at Desember, wondering what the hell they'd gotten themselves into.

"This is what I'm gonna do," the magistrate continued, "I'm gonna give you a two-thousand-dollar cash bond, each . . ."

Then she hit them with the whammy when she said, "I'm

going to implement a mandatory restraining order on the two of you for a period of four weeks. Maybe this'll give you kids a chance to think about something besides hitting each other."

"But we live together," Desember protested.

"Not for the next four weeks you don't."

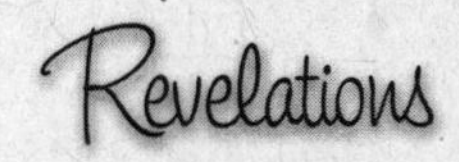
Revelations

12.

ICU

It was well into the wee hours of the morning when someone entered the chapel, snapping Desember out of thoughts of her and Fame's relationship over the past few months.

Despite feeling like ten-pound weights were fastened to her eyelids she raised them. Unaware of the hours that had lapsed since her arrival at the hospital, Desember tried to wipe the sleep from her tired eyes so they could better focus on the two people standing before her.

Her eyes adjusted to the light and as the two people moved closer, she recognized Nurse Shelia, who had given her the change of clothes, with a doctor wearing blue surgical scrubs in tow.

Desember thought maybe she should stand to hear what the doctor had to say, so she tried to rise to her feet. "Stay seated," the doctor said in the voice of a man who had been tirelessly working to save a life, or lives, all night and was inured to the long hours. She knew that he was there to bring her the information that she'd been anxiously awaiting . . . or maybe dreading.

Desember didn't know what to think. An array of emotions raced through her mentally and physically drained body: fear, hate, anxiety, and hope as she waited to hear what the doctor had to say. She studied his lips, and the words seemed to be coming out of his mouth in slow motion, maybe because she was so eager to hear what he had to say, words that would impact the remainder of her life.

"We removed the bullets but they caused a lot of internal damage." The doctor never lost eye contact with her as tears filled hers. "Because of the inflamed damage, we had to leave his abdomen open, which could cause infection."

A teardrop of happiness rolled down her face. He was going to live. *She knew it.* He was going to live!

"The next twenty-four hours are crucial. We're really worried about infection setting in."

Desember sobbed, but in her heart she felt the worst had passed.

"He's a real fighter," the doctor said, encouraging her hope.

"When can I see him?" she managed to ask him between sobs.

"He's going to be in the intensive care unit in a short while and you will be able to see him."

$ $ $

As soon as Fame was moved into the ICU, Desember sat patiently on one side of the bed, his mother on the other. Since

Francine still didn't know the details surrounding the shooting, she didn't have much to say to Desember, but she could sense that the girl loved her son.

At the twenty-fifth hour since the shooting, Francine asked, "Do you want to go to the cafeteria and get something to eat?"

For a brief moment Desember took her eyes off of Fame to address his mother. "No, ma'am, I'm good."

"Do you want me to bring you something back?"

"No, thanks. I don't have much of an appetite." Desember's stomach felt like it was tied in knots, and eating was the furthest thing from her mind.

"Well, I'm starving and need to smoke a cigarette." Francine grabbed her change purse, which seemed to double as a cigarette case, and began to exit the room. "I won't be long," she said, looking over her shoulder.

After a while Desember tried to concentrate on a crossword puzzle, but when she looked up and saw Fame's eyes flutter open, she rose, thinking that she was imagining things. His eyes looked weak, straining to focus, but it was a blessing that they were open. She was so excited to be able to face the love of her life again. His eyes searched hers. "I love you soooo much, Fame," she whispered to him.

With the breathing tube in his mouth, he could only give her a smile and a nod. He was trying to say something with his hands. "What's wrong, baby?" Desember asked, not wondering if the movement of his hand was a side effect of his surgery. Not knowing what else to do, she pressed the call button.

A nurse came in and checked his vitals. "Looks good. He's just regaining control of his muscles."

Once the nurse was gone, Fame's eyes never left Desember's, and it was clear he had something on his mind. With the index finger of his right hand and the palm of his left, Fame made a gesture as if he was writing. It clicked that he wanted something to write with. He was trying to communicate. She grabbed a pad and a pen off the bedside table and placed them in front of him.

He fumbled with the pen at first, dropping it, but after she put it back in his hand he began, a little shakily, to write something. When he was done she took a look:

U n danger!

And underneath that:

U gotta lay low!

She shook her head. "I'm not leaving your side."

But Desember knew Fame had a point. Until this moment, she hadn't realized she could be in danger. To be honest, she didn't care. She could take care of herself. All her focus was on Fame and him pulling through.

"Nothing's going to happen to me," she said.

He started writing again:

Can't take that chance. Love u 2 much!

His eyes were not trying to take no for an answer. The man could be so damn stubborn.

"Okay," she somewhat relented. Then she went on to tell him how the police and his family all thought she had something to do with the shooting.

He started writing again. She could tell it was taking a lot out of him, but he continued.

Don't TALK to police or no one.

"I didn't—and don't worry, I won't," she told him

Just then Francine walked in. "Oh my God, Famis. Thank you, Jesus," she said, her hands clasped together. "I was so worried about you."

Fame gave his mother a smile, then started laboring with the pad and pen again to resume the shaky writing.

"What's he doing?" his mother asked Desember.

"He can't speak yet," said Desember, "so he's writing what he wants to tell us."

This time Francine read the note:

Need ur help.

"Anything, son, you know that. What is it you need?" She was so excited that he was awake that she wanted to run out and get his siblings, but then she remembered that the doctor had made clear that no more than two people were allowed in Fame's ICU room.

They were both watching as Fame continued to scribble on the pad. This was the longest message yet. It took him awhile to complete it.

D is n danger. Watch her back. Nothing can happen 2 her. I love her 2 much. It will kill me.

Francine knew that Fame probably had a gut feeling that his brothers already had the girl's grave dug. She slowly nodded, with tears in her eyes, and then she took her seat by the bed as Desember stood at Fame's side. For the next couple of hours she watched as Desember administered tender loving care to her son.

Desember was gently wiping Fame's brow when he reached up and grabbed her hand. She had thought he was asleep.

Instead, Fame had been thinking about who his attacker might have been, but the exercise proved futile. He had gotten out on too many people, and now someone had caught him slipping. It was part of the game. Once he regained his strength, if he could put a face to the person, or persons, who had tried to assassinate him, he would look for his get back on general principles. But right now, while he lay helpless, his concern was for Desember.

He picked up the pen and paper and started to write again. When he finished he watched as Desember read the note.

U gotta get out of here. Not safe.

Francine read it with her. "I think he might be right," she agreed with her son."I will keep in touch with you."

Desember knew that Francine wasn't in her fan club, and Fame could see the hesitancy on Desember's face. He looked to his mother for reassurance.

"I will keep in touch with you, but it really isn't safe for you to be here."

Desember felt as if Francine was saying that for her own selfish reasons, but deep down in her heart, Desember knew it was the truth. It wasn't safe. They were unsure who had done this to Fame or if the same people would come after her, not to mention the police and his family.

The last note read:

Trust no 1!

D spent a little more time with Fame and then kissed him good-bye, not knowing if that kiss would be their final one.

13.

Daddy's Little Girl

As she exited Fame's hospital room, D had to face reality. She called her mother.

"Mom," she said when Angie answered the phone, "Fame's been shot . . . I'm okay . . . He should be okay too . . . I know you did, but now is not the time to remind me . . . Thank you . . . I just need you to come pick me up from the hospital."

About twenty-five minutes later a silver Volvo SUV pulled up in front of the hospital. Desember walked to the truck, got in and closed her eyes. She was dead tired.

"You okay, honey?" Angie was concerned. Desember looked a mess, like a runaway orphan who had been through fire.

"I'm not sure." Desember didn't look at her mother and spoke in a monotone. "Fame's afraid that the people who tried to kill him may come after me."

"Oh, my God. You have to tell the police about anybody that

would want to hurt him. Maybe they can pick up these killers before they try again, or even worse."

"What can be worse, Mom?"

Angie took a deep breath, then said, "They come after *you.*"

"Maybe I don't care if they come after me." Desember raised her voice to her mother. "How about that? Maybe I don't give a fuck."

"Then you're a stupid little girl. And I've known you to be a lot of things, but stupid was never one of them."

"I'm not stupid enough to marry a drunk asshole who beats on me anytime he gets the urge to drum on my face." Desember immediately felt bad for the low blow, but she wasn't going to sit back and let her mother verbally shove her around without pushing back.

"I'm the same stupid mother that always did whatever it took, even if it meant having her face drummed on, to make sure you never wanted for anything," she said solemnly.

"Everything but my real father," Desember countered, refusing to give in.

Angie ignored the statement—it was an old argument—and said, "I'll be the same mother that'll bury her daughter before her time."

They both had tears in their eyes now. It wasn't that they didn't love each other. Sometimes two people could look at the same picture and see different images. Position determines perspective.

"We all have to die one day." Desember was looking straight ahead, in deep thought. "It's one of the only guarantees in life," she said.

They were nearing the house when Angie said, "That's true, but only a fool would intentionally rush the process. It's not natural for a daughter to go before the woman that gave birth to her."

It was the longest forty-five-minute drive either of them had ever taken. When they turned onto Angie's block, there was a police car in front of her house. Joe ran out to the car the moment they pulled into the driveway. "Somebody broke out almost every one of the downstairs windows. This shit is fucking ridiculous!" he said at the top of his voice. "The police think that whoever did it may have been trying to send a message to *your daughter.*"

Joe seems more upset about the property damage than Desember's safety, Angie thought to herself.

Desember got out of the Volvo, walked up the steps and went in the house. There were two officers standing in the great room.

"How are you, Ms. Day?" one of the officers said. "If you don't mind, we would like to ask you a few questions."

"It won't take long," the other added. He looked like he would rather be somewhere eating doughnuts.

"Whatever happened here, I know nothing about it. I've been at the hospital all day, as I'm sure you probably already know. All I want now is to take a hot shower and get some rest. So you can go direct your questions to someone who may have some answers for you, because I have none." D stepped past the cops and went to her room.

Twenty minutes of tears mixed with the shower water made D feel slightly better, but she was still exhausted. She dried off and padded to her bedroom.

She could hear Joe and her mother arguing about what they should do. She guessed that with all the commotion, it must have slipped Joe's mind that the day before she'd held a knife to his throat.

"Do you know how much it's going to cost to get these windows replaced? They're top of the line," Joe said to Angie.

"Whatever the price, insurance will cover it. That's what we pay it for."

"*We* don't pay nothing; I pay."

"Whatever, Joe," Angie said, sounding frustrated.

"But she's bringing too much—"

"That's my daughter, not some—"

It went on for another ten minutes or so as Desember got ready for bed. She pulled the covers back and placed a small .22-caliber pistol under her pillow. She heard her mother talking to someone on the phone, but she couldn't make out what Angie was saying. Desember was too worn out to care, and her body only wanted to sleep.

Just as Desember was about to doze off, Angie came in her room, cutting on the light.

"Well," Angie said with a strange look on her face, "you're finally going to get what you've wanted."

"Right now, Mom, all I want is sleep."

Angie handed her a piece of paper with a name and an address on it. "Enough is enough. You're going to Richmond, Virginia, to live with your real biological father and his family until things cool off here."

Desember was stunned. "I'm going to live where?" She was sure she had misunderstood.

For as long as she could remember, she had been dreaming about the day she would finally meet her father. "Who is he, mom?"

Angie took a deep breath. "I don't know what he's doing these days, sometimes he's a hustler, sometimes he's a killer and, most recently, I heard he's a preacher." Angie sighed. "Everything you want to know about him he's going to have to share it with you himself. I haven't seen him in a long time. But you'll be safe with him."

Angie walked out of the room, but then turned around to add one more thing. "But I do know this for surc: throughout your life people could never understand why you had that innate need to hustle in you. Everyone knew that it didn't and could not have come from me. Clearly you got that from Des," Angie admitted as she chuckled a bit. "The truth of the matter is, you are a *Natural Born Hustler.*"

To be continued . . .

Acknowledgments

My grandmother Margaret L. Scott used to often say, "Every day with God is sweeter than the day before," and my life proves to be a living testament, the way God keeps blessing me beyond my wildest dreams. I have to thank God; it is because of him that I'm here, blessed and highly favored.

My two children—you are both growing up so fast—I truly am proud of you both and the young adults you are turning into. I thank you for being so understanding—and always a part of my "solution"!

Thanks to my family and friends who are supportive; you know who you are. Mom, the older my children get, the more I do understand and appreciate you and your sacrifices as a parent. My Craig—my ride or die! Aunt Robin for giving me insight about any and everything medical; Aunt Yvonne for always having my back—whether I'm up or down and most of all always having positive words . . . NO MATTER WHAT! My friend Mia Upshaw, for always being so understanding; Kia, for keeping me up on what I need to watch on reality TV. Tim Patterson, always keeping me level headed; EEM—your patience with me has earned you eternal respect and love. Marc for connecting the dots, and Melody for allowing me to take this from a brainstorm to pages. The entire Ballantine team for being so excited about the bridge that we have built!

To my undyingly loyal readers, thanks from the bottom of my heart for keeping my dream, hope, characters, and a world that I've created alive and vibrant! Without you none of this would be possible.

About the Author

Nikki Turner is a gutsy, gifted, courageous new voice taking the urban literary community by storm. Having ascended from the "princess" of hip-hop lit to the "queen," she is the bestselling author of the novels *Relapse, Ghetto Superstar, Black Widow*, *Forever a Hustler's Wife*, *Riding Dirty on I-95*, *The Glamorous Life*, *A Project Chick*, and *A Hustler's Wife*, and is the editor of and a contributing author to her Street Chronicles series. She is also the editor of the "Nikki Turner Presents" line, featuring novels from fresh voices in the urban literary scene. Visit her website at nikkiturner.com, or write to her at P.O. Box 28694, Richmond, VA 23228.